Tom

K. B. Sykes

North East Lincolnshire, England

www.kbsykes.co.uk

ISBN: 978-0-9556761-3-0

THURSDAY

The clouds rolled slowly across the waxing moon, blacking its silver glow to grey and adding to the increasing darkness. The close night air was silent save for the distant dull bustle of the people in the nearby town going about their late evening business on a crisp autumnal evening. A tense emptiness gripped the suburban street, undisturbed but for one shadow that weaved in and out of the gardens, searching.

He meandered along the pavement, attracted to the movements in the well-lit homes like an inquisitive moth to an enticing flame. Excitement rose as he watched silhouettes dancing on drawn curtains like a shadow puppet theatre, playing out their stories just for him. Thoughts of families gathered for evening meals and singles getting dressed and ready to hit the town in the hope of taking someone home. He looked up across the first floor windows in anticipation, naked shadows crinkled and blurred with steam. A dream of a young woman bathing stilled his gait and stirred his longing. He visualised her washing her delicate tender skin, almost in slow motion as the film played on in his mind's eye. The thought lingered seductively and he drew himself into the details of the soft female form in the privacy of his imagination.

Suddenly, he was snapped back into reality. A movement in a window, a pale coloured blur highlighted in his peripheral vision. With keen eyesight like that of an eagle, he turned to focus in on his mark. He waited for a moment by a hedgerow and looked over into the garden where the light cast down from the living room window brightened the lawn. Like a sinister fog weaving, his warm breath clouded slowly over the cold privet, whispering this way and that around the leaves until it faded into the air before being replaced by his next breath.

Exactly as he was hunting for, she came into view through the window, perfectly visible in all of her beauty in the bright light stark against the dark night. Butterflies danced in his stomach as he took a deep breath and smiled as tingles travelled up his arms and across his face. The curtains were wide and he had a clear view right through the house. He could see her walking in and out of the kitchen, pottering in the living room, picking up papers, a cup, the remote control, as she busied herself about her business.

Being sure not to enter into her line of sight, he savoured the view of her walking through the house in nothing but a dressing gown untied and open to reveal a tender young body in the prime of womanhood. Stroking his thigh with his trembling hand, his eyes narrowed, a thin smile crept up his cheeks and cut deep furrows into his jowls. For a few minutes he watched, with increasing breath, before nudging the gate open. He held onto the bolt so as not to allow it to make a noise. Just inside the garden he paused and backed up to the hedge avoiding the window's telltale light.

She had slipped out of sight. Where had she gone? Tense and anxious, he waited and quickly became angry as heat built up across his face and roared in his ears. How dare she disappear! A scowl grew across his forehead before being smoothed out peacefully when he saw her return to the room. Relief swept over him like a cool breeze on a hot summer's day.

Taking slow, deliberate steps, he advanced, carefully placing his feet down onto the pathway to minimise the sound of his shoes on the concrete. With his eyes fixed on her in the room he watched the gown wave with her movements as she walked over to an armchair and nestled in comfort. He got to the back door and pushed gently down on the handle. A muffled grind broke the final barrier between the predator and the prey. Through the narrowest gap he could afford, he slid himself into the kitchen, silent and slow. Music emanated from the room blended with her soft humming.

The heavy scent of perfumed soaps and shampoo hung in the warm air. He breathed quietly and deeply, feeding on the fragrance as his excitement rose. Stooping low to look around the base units through to the room, he surveyed his target, sat with one foot up against her thigh, holding her ankle with one hand. A soft naked breast exposed by the open gown, the nipple teasingly hidden from view. Longingly, his gaze followed the contours of her body and rested on a slice of pale, tender, inner thigh as it peeked seductively from the open folds of her robe. Long blonde hair, wet and glistening in the light, hugged her neck and snaked down over her shoulder. She toyed with the end, stroking it softly.

The tenderness of her long thin fingers invoked an uncontrollable shiver; a surge of arousal; a momentary lapse of concentration. He gathered his senses and calmed himself as he pushed the back door slowly in his white-knuckled fist. With his eyes tight shut, he eased the door back into place gradually and carefully. All the slightest sounds were drowned by the music and were barely audible in the charged air around him. Pause. Wait. Listen. All clear; he was in.

In a single quick stride, he crossed the kitchen unnoticed, passed the opening to the living room and out to the hall. In the dim shade he leaned back up against the wall, rested his hands on his knees and exhaled quietly before slinking along the wall to the bottom of the stairs. With movements so slow, so deliberate, he climbed, being extra cautious on his feet to reduce the risk of a creaking stair. Once at the top, he leaned back against the wall. Another controlled exhalation, a pause, a listen and he walked freely across the hall into the bathroom. He kept his steps light so as not to be heard from downstairs, although the sound of her singing gave him the confidence he needed to relax just a little.

The bathroom light had been left on and the window was steamed over with droplets cutting clear paths trough the condensation as they trickled onto the sill. There was a damp towel on the floor with two perfectly shaped wet footprints in amongst the damp patches. He imagined what she looked like when she had stood there, her naked flesh glistening, clean, scented and soft. Aroused, he shuddered.

Invited by a light streaking out across the floor from beneath a bedroom door, slightly ajar, he stepped lightly across the hallway. A low wattage bedside lamp was on which cast a large shadow of the uninvited guest across the wall and over the ceiling as he passed, like a sinister villain in a silent film. The unmade bed fired his imagination and he shivered at his visions. He kneeled, pulled the duvet to his face and rubbed against the cotton as he inhaled deeply. The stimulating odours of clean laundry, perfume and her naked flesh caused another surge of arousal. Standing at the dressing table, he gazed over a collection of small photographs alongside bottles of perfume. His reflection in mirror stopped him in his tracks. Momentarily startled, he pulled a crumpled, black ski mask from a pocket, opened it and slipped it carefully over his head. Now his reflection was as black as his shadow and revealed nothing but his piercing eyes.

He stepped over to a chest of drawers alongside the wall and gently pulled open the top drawer. Toying through the underwear and lingerie, he smiled and nodded to himself. Gently, he slipped the drawer closed and tried the one below it. There was a leather-bound diary, which on closer inspection held nothing but the dates of the owner's menstrual cycle and what looked to be appointments with various friends and relatives. Alongside, hidden slightly beneath a folded cloth, there was a small vibrator and a collection of sex toys. Wide and excited, he stroked the pink shaft of the rubber toy as he imagined the joy she must have felt as she played.

Taking his time, he looked carefully through the personal spaces within the most intimate chamber of the young woman downstairs. With delicate care and attention, almost with a deep respect, he dissected every slice of privacy. There was nothing to suggest a male presence in the house, no threat, nothing to fear. He stood with his dominance, silent in his supremacy, took a long look around the room, smiled to himself and clenched his fists. Slowly, cautiously, he opened a tall wardrobe door and browsed through the blouses and skirts. He took hold of a sleeve, rubbed it between his fingers and stroked the delicate material; the fine threads were as lace against the gravel of his roughened skin. Stealthily, without a sound, he dropped onto one knee and rummaged quietly through the shoes before pulling out a high-heeled, black leather boot. He raised the mask a little to reveal a thin, evil smile and then licked the boot from toe to top in one long, wet swipe. The earthy smell of the clean leather aroused him; his primal need beckoned him to touch himself, his patience and discipline ordered him to wait. With a need to control his tide of stimulation, he stroked the silver buckles with his thumb as if caressing sensitive skin. His excitement welled inside him, pulsating, throbbing and echoing his deep felt need for gratification. A sudden silence as the music downstairs stopped; the sounds of doors being locked and lights being flicked out stilled his desire. Lowering his mask, he put the boot back in the bottom of the wardrobe and stepped in, backed himself up amid the dresses and closed the door on himself.

Dark. Warm. Wait…

FRIDAY

The St Anthony of Padua Home for the Elderly stood proud in the centre of its formal gardens, almost castle-like, stout and square with outbuildings attached almost as an architectural after-thought. It was built of reclaimed, dull orange bricks with pale sandstone blocks around the doorways and windows, down the edges and across the gutter line. It was clean and new looking although the architect who designed it half a century ago had hoped to achieve the old fashioned Victorian look. A sandstone sculpture of St. Anthony of Padua stood over the main entrance, a Franciscan monk in a long robe, holding open a bible, as if for visitors to read. The formal grounds were neat; straight paths cut through closely mowed lawns and square trimmed hedges. The colourful flowerbeds had long since been cut back leaving nothing but the hardiest of shrubs in various shades of green and yellow. Along the paths there were benches, most of which had a small ceremonial plaque fixed to the backrest, fondly commemorating past residents.

The entrance hall was a fine and welcoming space. Yucca plants and bold ferns in large brass pots stood strong in corners. Great oil paintings of religious figures in various traditional scenes adorned the walls. It was bright and airy and lacked the odour often attributed to communal living homes for elderly people. The busy goings on that never seemed to subside, even at this early hour, created nothing more than subdued background sounds. Nurses walked here and there with a dull pad of comfortable shoes on the hardwood flooring. The lifts emitted a subtle ping that echoed inoffensively through the room as they opened their doors on the ground level. The broad staircase wound its way majestically along one side of the room with ornately carved balustrades casting long, pale shadows in the early morning sun.

Helen, a beautiful young woman with fair hair, dark eyes and fresh young skin walked along a wide corridor lined with large decoratively framed mirrors and oil paintings of once influential people. Smart and crisp in her uniform, she carried a wooden tray in one hand and looked at her watch on her lapel with the other. She paused by a door, tapped and waited for the "come in" from the other side.

"Morning Tom, how are you today?" she chirped happily with a smile.

Taking his daily paper off the tray, she folded it neatly onto the bedside unit, pulled his table across his bed with one hand, hindered only slightly by insubordinate casters. Tom sat up, still trying to shake his dreams from his cobwebbed mind, and pushed himself back onto his pillows ready for his breakfast. Huffing and puffing slightly more than necessary to ensure that he gathered her undivided attention, he sneaked a sideways glance as she leaned forward, trying craftily to catch a glimpse of breast, a lace strap or at least a tempting view of her sternum, but to no avail. The alarm clock on the side showed seven-o-nine. Helen was always decently covered and on time, give or take a minute or two.

"All the better now, thank you Helen. You know I dreamed again last night, about you I mean!" he smiled as he told her, nodding his head and raising his eyebrows.

"Behave Tom! We'll have none of that, people will talk," she joked as she gently pushed him forward a little and fluffed the pillows.

Neatly, she set his tray on his table before pouring a glass of water from the jug on his bedside and placing it next to a small plastic container holding his medication. He put the pills in his mouth one at a time and swallowed them down with a grimace before he turned his attention to the tray. The same breakfast everyday: One pot of tea, a glass of fresh orange juice, four rounds of buttered toast and a small pot of strawberry jam. For a frail old man he had a very healthy appetite. Helen turned to go as he picked up the knife and the pot of jam with a smile.

"Are you on your way already Helen? I thought we could chat for a while."

"Natalie called in sick this morning, Tom, so I'm taking some of her duties today. I'll pop back soon as I've finished," she replied as she pulled the door closed behind her.

Everything stopped for Tom as he watched her walk away from him. Shrugging his shoulders he tutted; rejected. For some reason, Helen brought back warm and comforting memories of childhood for Tom. Perhaps it was the way she smiled, or her perfume, or maybe even the sound of her voice. He often thought that she had the kind of voice that would narrate children's stories on television, the kind of stories with teddy bears, wellington boots and big adventures for little children. She had a subtle accent but he couldn't place it; he thought it was almost certainly Irish but then again it could have been Scottish though he knew little of national accents. He was sure that she had spoken to him of her childhood spent in open country, with clean air, full of life, rolling fields at the foot of great mountains and babbling brooks splashing through emerald woodlands.

"Could have been either, I suppose," he shrugged to himself.

Tom looked contentedly about his room while he ate his breakfast. It wasn't very big but since he spent most of his time in bed he didn't think that mattered. A walnut veneered wardrobe with a wonderful series of deep chestnut coloured rings on the doors often hypnotised him away from the endless repeats on television. He could let his mind wander for hours admiring those rings. Like a tank full of tropical fish or the dancing flames and embers of a real fire that had often kept his mind occupied in the past, he loved thinking while he gazed.

The chair looked out of place. It was modern, with no character and served only as a sensible seat for visitors. Tom often thought they were made deliberately uninviting so visitors would not get too comfortable and would leave a little earlier than they anticipated which made little difference to him, as he hardly ever had any visitors anyway.

The window was large with a panoramic view over the well-kept gardens and into the countryside beyond, but Tom preferred to see the sky. Looking at the sky gave Tom an excited, five-year-old-boy on Christmas Eve kind of feeling. He had always wanted to fly, to embrace the wind with both arms, roll out over the clouds and become a part of the eternal beyond. There was something about the attraction of the sky, flying, floating, dying. Tom found a great comfort in the prospect of death being so wide open and fresh, though the idea of any kind of judgement unnerved him. Longingly, he gazed out of the window up to the pale blue sky, scattered here and there with little white fluffy clouds, all levelled off at the bottom as if resting on an invisible table top. His mind wandered to days gone by when he could run, jump and shout. He saw himself playing as a child, running in slow motion through the cloudscape with the shouts of other children all around him, echoing in his mind.

When he had reduced his breakfast to an empty pot and a plate sprinkled with sticky crumbs, he pushed the table aside and switched on his radio. He unfolded the paper, took his spectacles from the bedside table and began to read. Now and again, he would talk to the radio, making comments about the singers or the articles in the paper. Suddenly, his door clicked and squeaked open slowly. A very round, wrinkled face popped in through the gap.

"You up for a visitor?" she croaked as she leaned heavily on her walking frame.

"All the time and any time for you my dear Elsie," replied Tom, folding his paper and returning it to the bedside unit.

"Come in and take the weight off your Zimmer!" he giggled.

He folded his spectacles onto the paper. It seemed to take ages for Elsie to get to the end of his bed. Tom just smiled politely throughout the strugglesome journey and became aware that he was deliberately holding onto the smile, as if he was attending a wedding and waiting for yet another photograph to be taken. She huffed, puffed and wheezed as she came, her eyes fixed on his all the while. She creaked on the walking frame and eventually dropped like lead onto the edge of the bed. She was a thin woman once, Tom thought, but the years had added to that, although not overly so. She always looked off balance, as if leaning over to the left, due to a mastectomy some years ago after a cancer scare. Her one remaining breast was ample for a woman of such a slight frame and did not flatter her posture at all. She wore bright red lipstick and blue eyeshadow, which Tom always considered somewhat odd, even on younger women.

"Give me a minute," she said, breathing heavily and with difficulty as she patted the bed beside her.

"You're looking particularly lovely this morning, Elsie, why you're positively glowing!" he paused and then leaned forward a little, "You got some new medication?" he joked.

"Cheeky sod!" she replied, "it's the walking makes me glow 'cause am knackered!" she wheezed as she laughed, which quickly turned into a kind of raspy cough.

She began telling Tom all about a new resident on the ground floor. She told him he had a nice backside and seemed to be here on his own as a single man, even though he was in a double room. Obviously, she was quite keen on him and Tom thought she knew an awful lot about him considering he had only been here a couple of days. Even though she was getting on a bit, Elsie never once considered herself as being 'past it', and often spoke about the male residents as if she were a schoolgirl on the lookout for a date.

"It's your birthday soon, innit Tom? How old you gonna be then?" she rasped, tapping his leg.

"On Tuesday next, so I'm told, but I can't remember how old I'm going to be. I lost track of the days when I retired, then the months went and the years had no significance after that. Last I knew the whole world was bracing itself for the big 'Y2K', which turned out to be a massive anti-climax!"

"Load a nonsense about nothing, that was, wannit?" she interjected.

"I don't care much for birthdays anymore, Elsie, I've had my fair share now," he added.

He looked down at his bed then out towards the sky. Elsie noticed and a fleeting thought of death scared her thoughts. She snapped herself out of it.

"We'll get something done for you though Tom. You deserve a bit of treatment you do," she nodded.

"Nothing too flash though Elsie, my dancing days are long gone!" he laughed as he pointed to the ceiling, disco style.

"And don't you go stripping for me either, Elsie – I couldn't handle that!" he laughed aloud and rocked in his bed, "and neither could you I bet!"

They joked and spoke, laughs consistently turning to coughs, until just before noon when Helen returned. She breezed into the room like a waft of fresh air, bringing the freshness of spring with her. Tom's face lit up and Elsie saw it. Smiling, she nodded and slowly drew herself up onto the walking frame. As she shuffled out, she amused herself as she imagined Tom attempting his carnal embrace with Helen; such a wrinkled old man and a beautiful young woman. She chuckled at her mental image, shrugging her shoulders up to her ears.

"See you later Tom. Enjoy your lunch," she said without looking back.

"Hey, Elsie, I'll be bringing your lunch today because Natalie is off. See you in two shakes," said Helen, swapping Tom's empty tray for a new one laden with a steaming hot meal and adding a magazine to his reading material.

"You coming to see me today or what then?" asked Tom; almost rudely as he stared at Helen's shapely behind in her crisp uniform.

Helen was taken aback by Tom's abrupt manner. She turned to speak but Tom interrupted her.

"I'm missing you, you know. I thought I'd have to do Elsie for a minute but I didn't think her lungs would be up for it!" he laughed himself into a cough again, this time it was quite a long cough and his face reddened.

Helen shook her head as she supported him back onto his pillows and handed him a small glass of water from the jug. Again he attempted to see beyond the apron and the white blouse beneath it but her naked beauty was still a secret to him.

"Tom!" she scolded, handing him the drink, "I said I would be here when I can. I have a job to do you know, I can't just entertain you all day," she smiled, although she was quite stern as she spoke.

When Tom was alone with his lunch, his focus wandered off to the clouds again. He watched them roll hypnotically across the sky as they changed shades and shapes and tumbled in slow motion through the air.

Life was good but desperately boring. The days were endless hours of pointless conversations and recitals of memories with temporary friends. He had almost resigned himself to his autumn years but his neglected libido and unrequited lust kept him hoping for something, though he didn't know what. And besides, something inside still wanted to kick out, to stick two fingers up to the world. Blank faced as he gazed through the window, he thought back to his exciting days and the times he had when he was fresh, youthful, vigorous and able. Faces of old friends, dead and gone, outlined in the clouds, their voices in his ears. The perfume of a favourite girlfriend, the warmth of her body on his, as real now as they had ever been, haunted him by their absence, teased his inability to remain fully erect. So many memories were bursting to get out, pushing against his forehead as they jostled for position in his mind. However hard he tried, he could not put them in sequence, or attribute them to a particular year. His grip on independence was slipping and life was becoming timeless. It would not be long before he became totally dependent on others and unable to think for himself. Remembering Elsie and the thoughts of next Tuesday, he tried hard to think how old he was but he struggled to put the years in order and he wasn't really sure what year he was in now. All he knew was that technology had overtaken his ability and the new fangled appliances were beyond his understanding. His head became heavy.

As the white fluffy clouds rolled across the sky and collected together as a looming grey blanket across the heavens, he began to remember darker aspects of his past and the unsavoury events that he had bottled away over the years. The memories he had tried to suppress rose to the fore and dragged red shadows across the walls. Darkness grew in the corners of his room like looming demons here to claim a soul in debt. Icy claws crept into the back of his mind and scratched into his thoughts. He rounded his shoulders and squeezed his head down. Blood pulsed in his ears, his chest tightened and his heart fought against the looming fear, which him into small swaying motions. As his peripheral vision faded, he slumped back onto his pillows and closed his eyes, surrendered to the red darkness patterned with jagged green hoops, concentric and swirling slowly away into the distance, hypnotic and mesmerising. Abstract images formed in his mind's eye like bitter and twisted psychedelic inkblots. He tried to ignore the images and their taunting, beckoning gestures. Desperately, he wanted to relieve himself of the burden of his unsettling memories so he could rest in peace with a quiet mind. He tried to calm the storm with colourful memories of happier, recent times. Thoughts of Helen; he could smell her scent and hear her voice. Whispering as if in prayer, he reassured and reaffirmed that everything would be all right and this whirlwind of anxiety would pass. Dark. Scared. Sleep.

* * * * *

He walked several paces behind her, watching her hips sway as she strolled along the high street looking in the shop windows. Now and again she would use her reflection to discreetly adjust her clothing or touch her hair but most of the time she browsed the sale items. He attempted to keep pace with her, his stride in time with hers. Several times he had to slow down to allow for the distance between them and intermittently, he stopped altogether, only to find himself staring indifferently at uninteresting products in the windows of shops he would never have visited. A distant onlooker, he admired her from behind and he imagined what she would look like if she turned around. She wore a short sleeved shirt - quite courageous as the weather didn't seem very reliable - with her coat draped over her arm, just in case. The narrow strap of her handbag cut through the diagonal across her back and the leather pouch with silver buckles bounced slightly against her thigh. Her short skirt, barely half the length of her thighs, had a slightly wider hem allowing it to sway with her movements, complimented her long, dark hair, plaited into a ponytail that swished behind her as she walked. Without tights or stockings, her naked legs with inviting smooth curves were accentuated by her sleek, high-heeled shoes. He imagined the soft delicate figure hiding beneath the expensive, tasteful threads that distanced her flesh from his touch. Wanting to break that barrier, he longed to get beyond the veil of dignity and experience her flesh, to reach out, caress her and own her. A swirling whirlpool of desire made him feel both anxious and energised as his obsession grew.

She was obviously interested in clothes and stopped at every opportunity outside shop windows to admire the latest fashions, at which point he would step into a doorway or turn around quickly, stare into shop windows or pace back and forth nervously. He must have looked suspicious to somebody somewhere but on a busy high street on Friday lunchtime nobody seemed to be paying him any attention. Suddenly, she began to fumble through her bag. Smartly, she picked out her mobile phone, which he only heard ringing after it had been exposed. With a forced smile she flipped it open. Her mouth moved but he couldn't hear her speak, and wondered who it might be. With a poisonous concoction of paranoia and jealousy his imagination created a handsome man with broad shoulders and a suntan; a heroic, strong man that could hold her and protect her, the kind of man that made him feel inferior, somewhat lacking and insufficient. Hatred grew. He despised him. With clenched fists by his sides and warmth swelling over his face, his temper boiled. How dare she allow another man to interrupt her while she was entertaining him?

Quickening his pace, his anger rose as he walked towards her with a determined stride. All other happenings in the street became a blur and the sounds became indistinct. As he drew near, a young boy ran across his path and caused him to stop in his tracks. With a sudden jolt back to focus, he realised that he was in the open, surrounded by people coming and going and couldn't possibly confront her here. He decided she could wait, he would tell her how he felt later. Like a retreating tide, his anger ebbed away and he calmed himself. He walked straight passed her with his head bowed and made his way towards a seated area outside a café. Once sat at a table, he turned to face her, lifted one leg across the other to rest his foot on his knee and leaned an elbow on the table. Somewhat angrily, he stared at her coming straight towards him, his bottom lip quivered for a moment and he realised his mouth was slightly open. He rubbed his chin as if to hide his expression and shook his head.

She had an oval face with a beautifully smooth jaw line, a slightly tanned complexion, thin lips and striking blue eyes. Her eyebrows and hair were deepest black and emphasised her features. In his imagination she was an eastern European, with an alluring accent and totally uninhibited. As he lingered over her body, soaking up the fluidity of her movements, he appreciated her slenderness, her body snaking hypnotically; her hips being the instigator of the rhythmic motion that held him in a seductive trance. Her breasts moved temptingly beneath her blouse, beckoning. She had put away her phone and was looking left and right as she crossed the street towards the café. For a moment he imagined that she was meeting him there and they would share a swift coffee before they moved on to a seedy room in a bed and breakfast down one of the many dirty side streets. He saw himself entwined with her, falling onto a bed as they tore at each other's clothes.

Aroused, he shuffled himself round to hide the obvious symptom under the table. He smiled at her though she never acknowledged him. Discreetly, he reached down under the table and touched himself from inside his pocket. He shuddered. With a deep breath he smiled again. This time she saw him and returned a quick, nervous smile before she dropped her eyes to the pavement. Without any further attention she walked by within touching distance. Her fragrance filled the air as she breezed passed and he inhaled deeply with his eyes closed. When he opened them again she had gone. A waiter arrived beside the table.

"May I take your order sir?" he anticipated politely with a pen and pad in his hands.

Without offering any form of response, he skipped up into the street, narrowly missing a shopper with heavy bags, and hurried off in the direction she had walked. Realising he was still erect he slipped his hands into his pockets to keep the bulge in his trousers from showing. There she was, beyond a crowd of people in the Market Square. Shoppers walked briskly this way and that like frenzied ants gathering food. She had stopped to talk to friends by a stall and was laughing in silence, her lips were moving but she was too distant for him to hear any sound. He stopped suddenly. Much to his surprise, a buggy scraped against the back of his ankles, bringing sensations of sharpness and warmth.

"Sorry!" said a young woman's voice, as she weaved the heavy pushchair around him without looking at him.

He glared at her, imaging all kinds of terror to unleash upon her inconsiderate soul, before looking back towards his European beauty but she had disappeared from sight. He scanned the horizon to no avail. Dejected. Busy people circled and complained at him for just standing in the middle of a busy street.

* * * * *

Helen came back after her chores had finished and all of her residents were settled in for the afternoon. Most of the nurses returned to the staff room to discuss their partners, children and last night's television. The same conversations took place during every break. Helen knew who would be sitting where and what they would be saying and doing. Although she sometimes enjoyed the pointlessness of small talk and the company of her peers was not altogether unbearable, she preferred to spend her free time with Tom. She liked Tom. He was kind, considerate and he listened to her when she was having problems. Often she had troubled him with her personal situations and asked him for advice. He was the nearest thing she had to a Granddad.

Her grandparents had died when she was young and she missed the relationship she used to have with her real Granddad. They lived in a big old house by the sea and she spent time there during the summer holidays. He used to take her for walks in the park or along the sea front. She remembered having to reach up high to hold onto his finger as she took extra large strides to keep pace with him. He always had a boiled sweet or toffee with him, which he would magically pull from her ear or out of her own pocket. The simple trick amazed her every time. She could still hear her Granddad's laugh as the sweet was revealed and feel the same thrill of excitement in her stomach.

She called Tom Granddad sometimes, when they were speaking together on serious matters, without the double-entendre wit that Tom was so fond of. He could be quite serious sometimes, although it was hard to tell with Tom. His sense of humour had at first lead Helen to believe that he was wholly inappropriate and didn't take anything seriously, but later events had proved her wrong.

Tom dragged himself away from his thoughts and opened his eyes when he heard the door click. Heavy rain pattered against the window.

"You OK, Tom? I didn't mean to wake you."

Helen sat in the chair next to the bed, like a family visitor to a sick relative in hospital. She sat on the edge of the seat and leaned forward with her elbows on her knees, shuffled a bit, felt uncomfortable and then decided to lean back and rest her elbows on the arms of the chair. That too was uncomfortable, so following some further shuffling she leaned over to one side. Tom smiled.

"Fine, Helen, I'm not asleep, just resting. It's a relief to see you actually; I was getting lost in my thoughts," he paused and drew a deep breath, "and I don't like that anymore" he added.

"I'm trying to put my memories into some sort of order," he continued, "have a good old clean out, you know. Have you got my date of birth on your records?" he asked.

"I'll look it up for you Tom. It's your birthday on Tuesday isn't it? Have you had a telegram from the Queen yet?"

"I don't think so," he shook his head slowly, and after a slight pause added, "I've got so much building up inside me Helen; I need to get it all out. Such a long life fills your head with memories and I can't carry it all anymore."

His voice sounded low, as if he was tired. His usual enthusiasm had vanished.

She replied reassuringly, "I can listen to your stories all day," with a broad smile.

Tom told Helen all about his 14th birthday, or it might have been his 12th. He told how his friend Simon, or it could have been Dave, got himself stuck in the railings at the park while trying to sneak through a fence to retrieve a stray football. The rest of the party guests had taken the opportunity to throw cake and sweets at him while he was stuck. The Fire Brigade had to come out to cut him free and his father had beaten him for it when he got him home. Tom found the whole thing very amusing. He expressed himself so fully when he told his stories. His tone of voice, his gestures, his whole body got involved. Sometimes he would glaze over, as if he was no longer in the room but had drifted elsewhere, seeing the visions he was speaking of, becoming lost in his own story. Helen imagined he would have made someone a wonderful father, telling bedtime stories with such commitment. His face was old and well worn but so full of life. When he spoke, his eyes sparkled, and betrayed him when he tried to hide his feelings. Helen could listen to him for hours, if she had the time, but alas today, she did not. It was getting on for teatime and the residents would be expecting their visits.

Helen thought she could slip out unnoticed when Tom was lost in the middle of one of his stories but she could never be that rude. She waited for a lull in the story, which never came, but then Elsie appeared at the door. Her interruption caused a cessation for Tom, which gave Helen a convenient moment to make her escape. Elsie wheezed as she slowly made her way over to Tom before she slumped down on the foot of the bed. She rasped and gasped, wide eyed for a short while with one hand on her chest while the other held on to her walking frame. Tom seemed to be gently smiling at her, although in his mind he was still laughing at his young friend stuck in the railings splashed with icing and jam. Elsie smiled gently back.

She began to explain that her niece, Jodie, was coming over to see her with her baby. Tom hadn't returned from his party in time to catch the first couple of sentences but heard enough of the conversation to fill in the bits he'd missed. Unfortunately, Jodie's no good partner was coming too. Elsie had raised her niece from a very early age, when her sister and brother-in-law where killed in a tragic road accident. Jodie had been in the car too but she survived without a scratch, although she had no memory of the event at all. Jodie couldn't even remember her parents, or at least not enough to be emotionally scarred by the loss. Tom had heard the story at least twice, but he let her tell it again anyway.

"She must have only been about two years old, if that," explained Elsie, "poor thing."

Jodie was a very pleasant girl, as Elsie was so fond of telling people, but a little bit gullible and lacking in common sense even though she had spent some years at university and done very well for herself, getting her degree in some 'ology or other. Elsie couldn't remember what it was, but she was very proud of her little niece. According to Elsie, Jodie could have done a lot better than Graham. She called Graham a sly devil, out for what he could get. He could "charm the knickers of a nun" so Elsie said, and he had charmed her dearest niece into starting a family and allowing him to stay in it. He wasn't really interested in having a family; Elsie knew that much and insisted on making it known to all that would listen. She believed that Jodie had fallen pregnant by mistake and Graham had just seen an opportunity to stick around and milk her for all she was worth; to secure himself an easy life from Jodie's inheritance. Elsie had amassed quite a fortune over the years and Jodie was the only beneficiary. Graham knew that, Elsie maintained, because he could "smell money a mile off".

When Elsie spoke about the baby, Connor, she smiled and talked with a higher tone, as if she was talking to a baby. She described him in detail and likened various features to those of relatives of hers. She often complimented him on his handsomeness.

"But I don't like the name," she said "Connor – it's a last name really don't you think Tom?"

Tom had been listening politely all the while and only nodded now and again with an occasional "hmmm" or a quick smile.

"I suppose it was a trendy name when he born," he replied after a thoughtful silence, "one of those names that will only come around now and again. But I dare say you'll get used to it, if you're calling him that all the time it will grow on you," Tom nodded and smiled reassuringly.

Helen appeared at the door with a smile and tea tray. Elsie made her excuses to leave, huffing and puffing as she climbed up to her frame and shuffled out of the room. She slowly vanished off down the corridor. The fading sound of her rasping breath in time with the walking frame tapping on the hard floor brought a smile to Tom's lips. Helen had arrived in the room like a strong spring zephyr gusting about; task focussed and determined to do exactly what she needed to in the shortest possible time. She poured the tea and added the milk without talking. She was obviously in a hurry.

"Still busy, Helen? Poor you. Have that young man of yours take you out this evening. Tell him I'll have words with him if he doesn't!" Tom said, getting louder as Helen vanished out of sight.

In her haste, Helen had left the door to Tom's room wide open and he could see out into the corridor. With the doors being wider than average for wheelchair access, the corridors being well lit and having mirrors to reflect the light, the view through an open door could be quite extensive. There was a pretty young nurse there, leaning on her shoulder against the wall, her legs crossed at the ankles. She toyed with her hands and turned the rings on her fingers. She was obviously enjoying talking to someone but he couldn't see whom. It was a man's voice; he was flattering her and being very friendly.

Tom screwed up his eyes and leaned forward slightly to edge in on the conversation. He heard him compliment her on her appearance and ask her some insignificant questions about her tastes in food and music. Tom chuckled to himself on hearing some of the same old lines that he himself had used so many times.

"I can't believe he used that one. It was already old when I was young!" he smiled and spoke in a humorous tone, although a slight hint of jealousy surfaced from deep within.

She was answering all the questions with a smile and an occasional giggle. Tom sat back on the bed and laughed a little laugh. He looked up in time to see the nurse hand the man a small piece of paper and then vanish off down the corridor to the right. Seconds later the man passed the door in the opposite direction, half walking, half running, as if catching up to where he should have been had he not been distracted by the pretty young nurse.

"Some guys have all the luck!" Tom tutted and shook his head.

* * * * *

Elsie was sitting in her 'bionic chair'. She called it that because it had a mechanism that could raise and lower the seat to make getting in and out easier. It whirred and vibrated a touch as it moved slowly from one position to the next. Elsie was no longer physically able to enjoy the slight vibrations but she was very grateful that the cushion could get up to meet her bum rather than her bum getting down to meet the cushion.

All of Elsie's furniture had extra fittings and features to make them user-friendly for the less-abled individual. Her bed had a control panel on the side to adjust the height and angle of the mattress. It split three ways and each section could be raised or lowered as desired. All of her cupboards had extra grip attachments on the handles and the rails on which she hung her clothes could be pulled down with a short pole to make them easier to reach and to hang her clothes.

She sat in her chair with her ankles crossed in front of her as she silently gazed over a magazine. Fantastic tales of celebrity marriages and break-ups and how ordinary people had experienced extraordinary things kept her attention as she shrugged and smiled her way through the pages. She never read the stories thoroughly; only skimmed over the headline and the top paragraph or so. She licked her finger to flick the pages over, skipping some here and there, and paused over the puzzle page.

"Paranoia," she said, out of nowhere, before scribbling on the page with her pencil.

"Beg pardon, Aunt Elsie? What you say?" Jodie had appeared in the doorway, smiling, "Who told you I was paranoid?" she joked, looking left and right as she walked in the room, ducking next to the bed and turning around quickly to press her back up against the wall.

"Seven across!" laughed Elsie, "Paranoia!" she tossed the magazine aside and pressed a button on the arm of the chair.

The chair started to whirr and Elsie was elevated into a standing position. She met Jodie in a hug and rested her bum against the cushion. She was back to being seated after another short whirring sound.

"It's so good to see you my dear. Where's Connor?" she questioned, looking past Jodie, expecting the little pushchair to appear in the doorway with 'him' pushing behind.

Jodie explained that Connor was at playgroup and she'd be collecting him later. She spoke proudly of all the pictures he had painted and the new nursery rhymes he had learned with all the hand movements. The pictures were in the back of the car and she would let Elsie have one for her room.

"That would be nice to brighten this place up a bit. Thank you," smiled Elsie.

"Graham's around somewhere, he said he would meet me here straight from work. He isn't here though is he? Probably gone to the loo."

Jodie looked around the room as if she was searching for him, but he was obviously not there. Elsie shook her head lovingly at her niece's silliness.

Elsie and Jodie chatted for a few minutes about the change in the weather, the playgroup and the new neighbour with the nice backside until Graham appeared at the door. Elsie had seen him out of the corner of her eye and rolled her eyes discreetly.

"Hello Aunt Elsie, how you doing?" he leaned over to kiss her cheek and Elsie grimaced as she turned her head away.

Jodie and Elsie chatted some more with very little acknowledgement of Graham's presence. He had come to accept this from Elsie and resigned himself to second best in these situations. With a sigh of rejection, he sat himself down on the edge of the bed with a forced smile. He pushed his spectacles up on his nose as his eyes wandered about the room as he tried really hard to find something to occupy his mind. He curiously pressed one of the buttons on the panel next to him and felt a cushion inflate just behind him. The sudden hissing of air startled him and he quickly let go of the button. Elsie and Jodie instantly turned and stared him. He smiled nervously by way of an apology for temporarily breaking the flow of conversation, and then he made a noise in his throat and took a deep breath. He continued to nod now and again and made very little contribution to the conversation until he finally chipped in,

"We better go and get Connor now, darling. We don't want to be late."

He tapped his wrist where his watch would have been if he had been wearing one, and pushed his glasses up higher on his nose as he stood up.

Elsie smiled all over her face as her chair rose up, slowly. Jodie said her goodbyes and gave Elsie another big hug and a little kiss on the cheek. Graham stepped in for a hug but the reverse journey to the seated position had already started so he awkwardly changed his footing and turned to leave. He raised his arm around the back of Jodie's waist. Elsie just looked at him, straight mouthed. He knew she didn't like him, she knew he didn't like her and Jodie was oblivious to the mutual, awkward relationship. Elsie muttered mild obscenities under her breath as they faded away down the corridor. She looked over to her magazine and contemplated getting up out of her chair to retrieve it from the floor. After careful consideration, she decided it was too much trouble to get up just for the magazine and thought she might go for a short walk as well. She had a gadget for picking things up off the floor hanging on the wall where she could reach it easily. Elsie thought it was a great thing to have. She pulled the trigger and watched the two fingers come together in their pinching motion while she imagined the new inmate's shapely bum. She chuckled to herself, retrieved the magazine and placed it on the arm of her chair. On her way out, she hung the stick back where it belonged and muttered under her breath again.

* * * * *

Tom was still drinking his tea when Elsie came in and plonked herself down on his bed with the usual breathing display. Tom had to pull his feet away sharpish to avoid the squash. Elsie gave Tom a look that immediately made it clear to him that she needed to have a good moan, so he leaned back on his pillows, folded his hands on his lap and waited. Elsie took a deep breath before she dived in, building up her reserves in preparation for a long talk. She started with the background of Graham and Jodie, which Tom already knew, but he excused this waste of his time by trying to convince himself that this was a good recap. She went on to explain the mutual disliking between her and Graham, and her suspicions of his character. She took great pleasure in pointing out his flaws with a passion matched only by fanatics raving on about their truest loves in life. Tom wondered if there was any Freudian philosophy going on but after he had considered the relationship between Elsie and Graham he decided against the idea. He concluded that she really did hate him and it wasn't some unrequited love, although it was possible that Graham would have been the kind of man that Elsie would have found attractive in her youth. Elsie's mouth was still moving and her eyes were fixed on Tom, so he dragged himself away from his thoughts and nodded, just in case. Elsie was still explaining that her and her husband had never wanted children due to their work commitments. She was a technological adviser with a large electronics firm and he was a detective with the local CID. They both worked long hours as they chased their retirement funds and climbed their individual corporate ladders. Elsie explained that her way of life had to change dramatically when her sister was killed and she took Jodie into her care.

Helen came in and sat down without interrupting. Elsie was saying how she had never regretted not having children. She treated Jodie as her own and was devoted to her. Helen spoke about her plans for the future with Nathan, who she loved deeply; judging by the look in her eyes when she spoke of him. Elsie was very interested in things like the colour of his eyes, his inside leg measurement and skills in the bedroom, though Helen wasn't comfortable with the questioning and dismissed them instantly. She decided she would like to have children in five years or so, after she was fully trained and Nathan had developed his career. He part-owned a small computing company. He sold webspace and built network systems for large organisations but actual work he did was unknown to Helen, and not entirely understood by Tom or Elsie, who just frowned and nodded. Helen could see she was losing them and was not at all confident in explaining things she did not fully understand, so she fell silent and shrugged her shoulders.

"I had a child once, so I was told" stated Tom in a flat, matter-of-fact tone.

Helen and Elsie were shocked. This had never been mentioned before, not even hinted at. After they had looked at each other aghast, they turned to face Tom, but he began talking before either of them could express their surprise.

"I never knew at the time," he said in a questioning tone, "she was just a girlfriend I had once, nothing serious really. I only knew her for one summer; I think her name was Mandy, or it could have been Mary. Only got with her because of her talent with her tongue, if you know what I mean. What she couldn't do wasn't worth doing!" he smiled a slight laugh.

"I found out I had a kid years later by chance. A mutual friend of ours had mentioned that she had a kid some time after we split up and the alarm bells had rung in my head. I did the maths and got excited. I quite looked forward to meeting my child, you know. I would have liked that. He told me where I could find her so I went round a few days later."

Tom paused and his tone lowered as sadness grew in his eyes. Helen and Elsie were gripped.

"She had really lost it by then. She used to be so pretty; chestnut hair, green eyes, beautiful smile...."

He trailed off into a fond memory. Helen could see her as well as he could. He painted the picture so well. He explained about her love for life and how she danced her worries away in the nightclubs. She had wanted to explore the world, discover new things and have as many exciting experiences as she could before she got too old. Elsie liked the sound of this girl; she was just like she used to be. Elsie tried hard to listen, but her tiredness had been flowing in for some time and she drifted into a sleep filled with dreams of exciting youth.

"When I saw her at the door I could see life had kicked her in the teeth and her dreams had been shattered. She was bedraggled and filthy."

Tom's face was scrunched up and his mouth had turned down at the corners,

"Her hair was a mess. She was wrinkled. Turns out she'd taken to drugs after having the baby and lost the plot a bit. What a waste of space she had become. Scum, really."

Tom trailed off and moved about on his pillows. He pointed in silence to the sleeping Elsie, who had rested her chin on her chest and only grunted occasionally. Helen looked and smiled. Tom reached for his tea, took a sip or two and put it back on the side. He wiped his mouth with his fingers and turned to look at Helen.

"She was pointless now, you understand?" his voice was ominous.

Tom looked directly at Helen with raised eyebrows, waving his hand in front of him.

"She had lost the will to live but was too afraid to die. And what's more, she'd had my baby and given it up!" he sounded genuinely cross, a tone that gave Helen a sense of fear.

The pulsing in his ears began and his peripheral vision clouded red. As his voice grew louder, Elsie murmured her way to the surface of her sleep and shook her head, then fell deeper into her slumber. Her chin dropped onto her chest causing her to rock forward slightly on the bed and her breathing whistled through her nose. Tom closed his eyes and shook his head slowly from side to side until his neck clicked.

"She told me all about the baby," he explained, rubbing the back of his neck, "She insisted it was definitely mine, she had no doubt about that but when she had it her go-getting friends left her behind. She couldn't be cool and travel the globe with a screaming shit machine in tow could she? She blamed me for everything, started shouting at me about how it was my fault she got pregnant in the first place … if that hadn't happened then she wouldn't have lost her friends … she wouldn't have turned to drugs … and on and on and on ... She let me have it that day, both barrels! I kept getting angrier and angrier; I could feel myself getting hotter."

Tom gritted his teeth and shook his hands in front of him as gripping someone by the lapels.

"She was in mid-rant when I slapped her. She fell silent instantly and just stared back at me. Then out of nowhere, she slapped me back just as sharp. I hit her again. And again. Two loud smacks and then she fell onto the couch. She picked up her cup of coffee from the table and threw it in my face! Bitch! Good job it had been there a while and wasn't too hot. I hit her again and then grabbed her by the throat. I lifted her right out of her couch and onto her tip-toes."

He was smiling again, miming the strangling action with one hand out in front of him as he grasped an invisible neck,

"I was surprised how strong I was," he sounded quite proud, "I squeezed her throat tight and she went red. Then blue. She soon got too heavy so I had to let go. She fell back on the couch, holding her throat and gargling a bit. The look of fear in her eyes was priceless; it turned me on."

Helen shuffled in her seat, uncomfortable in the chair and by what she was hearing. Her face had paled and she felt her stomach fluttering. She looked over to Elsie, hoping for support, but she was still asleep, smiling to herself, dancing on a distant shore with a handsome stranger.

"I could have killed her right then," Tom continued, "but I noticed some kid hanging around outside, looking in from the street and pacing up and down. I remember being quite scared then, all of a sudden like. I went over to the window, pulled back the net curtain a bit and had a look. He turned and looked just as I dropped the curtain back. I didn't think he'd seen me."

He reached over for his tea and took another sip. He held on to the tea in his lap, both hands wrapped round the cup. Elsie made a grunting sound in her throat, shuffled a bit, and continued to sleep. Helen was hoping for Elsie to wake, to create an excuse for her to leave. She was becoming agitated by the story and did not know where to put herself or what to feel.

"He stood staring for a while but I think he was probably a customer, wanting a fix, or sex. When I saw him leave, I turned back to her. She had straightened herself up and was preparing a needle. I could smell the smoke coming from the spoon as she heated it up. It smells foul you know! You never forget that smell. She was just about ready to put the needle in her arm when I got to her. I took it off her, she didn't fight, she just looked at me, scared, then she looked away. I think she thought I was going to hit her again. I looked at the syringe and noticed a few air bubbles in the shaft," he paused and sighed.

"She'd obviously not done it right. Maybe she was scared, maybe she was thinking about something else, I don't know. I think I would have loaded it with some more of that filth but then I could see I didn't have to. Once those air bubbles get into your bloodstream..." he paused, "she stared at me in silence, whacked up and fell back. She twitched a bit and then lay there, unnaturally still, with her eyes open. She was found dead some time later by some kid; another customer. I read it in the newspaper."

Tom placed his cup on the side and lay back on his pillows. He looked up at the ceiling with an empty expression.

"Never will know about my child now. Not even if it was a boy or girl. Couldn't even guess at an age. Strange that is. I've often wondered."

He closed his eyes as a single tear trickled out of the corner of his eye, across his cheek and down onto his collar. Helen watched it roll; the silver trace caught the light, a whirlpool of blended sadness and loss reflected in that tear just for a moment. She sighed heavily and looked up at Elsie, who was shaking her head and yawning. Tom was falling asleep, so it seemed. His eyes were closed and his breathing was relaxed and deep. The veins in his neck and forehead were raised slightly. He rolled his head over to the side with his mouth slightly open.

Helen wiped her face with her hands and blinked hard before she stood up. She took a deep breath, brushed down her apron and straightened her hair. She took a moment just to stand still and gather her thoughts before she ushered the waking Elsie up on to her frame and walked with her out of the room. She turned back to look at Tom from the doorway; he was motionless with the feint trace of that tear down his cheek.

When she got back to the staff room she paused in the fading light. She sat on the old, well-worn couch and sunk back into the cushions. Staring at nothing, she wept, sobbing silently with lonely tears running down her face. Feeling vulnerable, like a child, her hands were shaking and her fluttering stomach had knotted. The cold of the room somehow itched under her skin. She wrestled with her thoughts as she tried to put Tom's story into perspective. The questions were arguments in her mind that wailed on and on and beckoned an atrocity of nightmares as she faded into a disturbed sleep.

When she awoke, uncomfortable and rough, her make-up had blackened her cheeks and her nose was running. The soft evening sunlight broke through from behind the diminishing rain clouds and gently filtered in through the blinds on the window. She wrapped her arms around her middle, held herself tight and keeled over to her side.

* * * * *

He returned to the Market Square where he had last seen his European beauty. Deeply disappointed that she was no longer there, although he had hoped she would be, he never really expected her to be. There were very few people about. Most of the shoppers had taken shelter from the rain and had not returned after it had stopped. The stallholders were packing away their wares and rolling down the shutters on their shops. Some younger, louder party-seekers were meandering towards the pubs and clubs in the town centre and taxicabs bustled up and down the roads surrounding the square. He walked slowly along the drying pavements, hoping to find her again. With his hands in his pockets he stroked himself as he remembered her. In his mind's eye he replayed his imaginary encounter, rolling in the sheets of a cheap bed and breakfast room, stained with the seeds of their excitement and paused momentarily to shudder at the enticing thought. Slowly, warmly, he rubbed and squeezed his pulsating manhood through his pockets as he walked, quickening his pace as his excitement rose. Short of the climax to his pleasure, he stopped and allowed himself a moment to relax. He continued with the pattern, masturbation and relaxation, as he walked around the periphery of the Market Square. The intensity of his orgasm increased every time he neared ejaculation and he knew that when he did release it, it would be strong. He controlled his urge and waited.

A bar had opened on the edge of the Square and a few early drinkers had started to congregate around the entrance. Scantily clad females giggled their way to the doors, much to the delight of the burly bouncers and eager young men that waited for them. He looked the girls up and down, with their provocative clothing and tempting behaviours, convinced that they wanted him. Toying with himself, he brought himself as close to climax as he dared. Across the street, several young women came towards the Square and walked closer to him. He stood and stared into the eyes of a young brunette and shivered as he ejaculated into his trousers. His knees trembled and he groaned quietly. Buckling under pleasure, he stumbled on his feet. The young woman was an arm's length away from him and nudged her closest friend to get her attention. She pointed out a dark patch on his trousers where his semen had dampened them from inside and the two girls laughed at him. They giggled to their friends and they all turned to point and stare. Anger fired up inside him suddenly as he realised what was happening. They should not be laughing at him, they should be admiring him. They should be respecting him. He scowled at the girls as his fury rose to boiling point, his vision clouded over in a red mist and he struck out with his fist. Hatred guided his hand though he made only a weak contact with the first of the girls as she flinched to avoid the force of the blow. A second girl stepped forward and swiftly aimed her high-heeled, pointed boot towards his genitals. With a scream and a barrage of abuse, they spat and hit at him. Overwhelmed, bruised and sore, he turned and ran away to the sounds of jeering and name-calling wrapped in high-pitched laughter.

By the time he had fled the Square and entered the side streets, the damp patch on his trousers had gone cold and begun to harden. Short of breath, he ducked into an alleyway and rested against a wall, where the sounds of somebody singing in a garden behind him invited his attention. He turned to a hole in the rickety wooden fence and saw a young woman wearing headphones, walking up and down the garden path, smoking. He quickly scanned the back of the house; there was no sign of anybody else at home. Quickly, violently, he burst through the already damaged gate. The singing stopped and he was upon her before she could scream. He wrapped an arm around her neck and covered her mouth, dragged her back out into the alleyway and banged her head against the fence, and then swiftly he swung her across the alley and pushed her against the wall. She cried and struggled all the while, biting at his hands, kicking at his legs, scratching at his face, though he was indefatigable. Again he bashed her head against the wall. Her struggles subsided and she went limp in his arms. Cautiously, he looked down the length of the alley to the streets at either end before he gently lowered her onto the floor and removed her leggings and her knickers in one swift pull. She murmured as he rubbed her pubic hair with his rough hand and his fingers found their way in. He pushed against the dryness and spread his fingers inside her. He had just begun to unbutton his trousers when a loud shout startled him. Instantly, he rose to his feet and ran down the alley to the street beyond.

SATURDAY

Elsie woke in the morning nice and early without the aid of an alarm or wake up call as she always did. She pressed the buttons on her bed and lowered herself down to within easy reach of her walking frame. On her way past the window, she pulled the cord that opened the blinds, letting in the first few rays of sunlight on this new dawn. As she removed her nightwear, she chuckled to herself and shrugged her shoulders up to her ears as she found her thoughts amusing. Using anything she could to rest on, she made her way into her bathroom and sat down on a plastic seat under the showerhead. It was always cold, that seat. She had tried to turn the shower on first to get the whole thing warm but the floor had become too slippery for her liking and she wasn't so confident on her feet in the wet. With her eyes closed and her skin up in goose bumps, she nervously twisted the tap. The sharp water hit her skin like a thousand fat needles and never failed to startle her. The initial tension caused by the sudden cold was over quickly and Elsie soon got warm. With a sigh of relief she raised her head to let the water flow down her face. She urinated in the shower, letting it trickle through the gaps in the chair as she did every morning. With the minimum of effort, she washed quickly and then brushed her teeth with the shower still running. The main support bar had been installed just slightly out of reach and Elsie found herself having to fall onto it rather than grab it as she stood up, which was a little more than she was comfortable with. Muttering under breath, she splashed her way out of the bathroom, swinging from one handle to the next like an asthmatic gibbon as her hands slipped a little on every handle she grabbed. Finally, with a mild sense of achievement, she landed on her walking frame with a sigh of relief. Taking a towel from the rail, she wrapped it rather awkwardly around her distorted figure. She giggled and shrugged, lifted her frame out in front of her and tried to use one of the front feet to turn on her radio; it saved her leaning over. After several badly aimed taps, Elsie concluded that silence was golden and the radio could wait. The towel slipped off around her feet and Elsie laughed.

In the mirror across the room she caught sight of her naked body and was thankful for the steam and her degenerating eyesight that obscured the true horror of what was once a beautiful young form. She stooped to pick it up and promptly broke wind on her way down, which started her laughing again which made it difficult for her to rise. When the laughter turned to a cough and the cough had subsided to heavy breathing, she dried herself thoroughly. Although her body was old her mind was young. Humour was a good friend to Elsie and she could laugh at herself without resentment. She opened her wardrobe and took out a small tube of talcum powder, her make-up bag and began to thumb through her clothes. Her outfits were neither fashionable nor glamorous, but she still took pride in her appearance. She went over to her bionic chair, still in the raised position, as it always was when she wasn't sitting in it, and made herself comfortable before getting herself ready for the day. It wasn't long before Natalie came in with her breakfast and a cup of tea.

"Morning Elsie, sleep well?" Natalie asked.

"Oh yes love thanks. You feeling better today are you?" replied Elsie.

"Yes thanks. To be honest Elsie, I only had a hangover yesterday but don't let on you know, OK?" Natalie gave a sly smile and slight tilt of the head, "Friend of mine's birthday so we had a girls' night out."

"OK love. Safe with me, know what I mean?" Elsie tapped her nose with her finger and laughed, "You sound like I was you know. You like to party do you, Nat?"

"All the time." smiled Natalie with a wink.

Elsie liked Natalie. She was a feisty young girl who liked to dance all night given the opportunity, just like Elsie in her youth. A lover of fun, and often mistaken for being an 'easy girl', though the truth of it was she just liked loud music and alcohol; one night stands were not on her agenda, much to the disappointment of the on-looking boys. Elsie fancied herself as a bit of a Natalie type, though in reality she was more inhibited than she liked to believe and not quite as wild as she told others, but that didn't make her any less of a party lover.

Natalie walked in a way that made men watch her. Whatever it was that made men want her, serve her and pay her attention, she had it in abundance; charisma, mystery and a shining personality. With a well-formed figure, tight where it needed to be and rounded in the most inviting of places, she was always well presented. Elsie liked to think that she once had the power to turn men's heads, and for a while in her peak of youth, she did. Natalie left the room and Elsie tucked into her cereal. No sooner had she finished than Jodie and Connor appeared in the doorway as Elsie wiped a trickle of milk from her chin with a tissue. Jodie was fluttering excitedly; she could not keep still for a minute.

"He's done it, Aunt Elsie, he's gone and done it!" shivered Jodie, almost jumping up and down.

"Who's done what?" asked Elsie "he hasn't left you for another woman has he?" although Elsie saw the new ring on her finger and braced herself.

"Quite the opposite! He's proposed to me! He wants to marry me this summer! How great is that?" Jodie thrust out her hand to show off the diamond.

Elsie thought it was beautiful ring; he had chosen well and should be commended for that, though her heart sank as she sensed his temporary victory. Her whole body slumped down deeper into the chair but Jodie didn't notice; she was giddy with happiness. Jodie explained that Graham had stayed out all night with a friend, to get some time alone and reassure himself that he really loved her. Apparently he had been discussing his decision all night through and had come to the decision to ask her to marry him. Elsie shook her head slightly in disbelief, sucking through her teeth with a clicking squeak. Jodie appeared so excited but then what could Elsie do? Deep down, her instincts told her that this was wrong and she had to tell Jodie, but not right now, not in the heat of her excitement. This called for a special blend of tact. Jodie was fragile, emotionally speaking, and any kind of discomfort had to be revealed gently, with care. Elsie thought it best to remain as neutral as possible, to offer support without actually agreeing to the marriage. If she could postpone giving her blessing for long enough, Graham would reveal his true colours before the big day arrived. If he did not, Elsie decided she would expose him in time to save her niece.

"Well we'll look forward to the summer then, shall we?" she looked at Jodie, still toying with her ring and admiring the gemstone in the light, and tried to smile convincingly, "What's that you've got there, Connor?"

Surprisingly successfully, Elsie changed the subject and got to play with Connor for a while. He was pulling crayons and paper out of a little ladybird shaped bag he had with him, happy in his own little world, oblivious to the big decisions going on around him. Swiftly, Jodie picked him up, which he made known was against his wishes, and placed him on Elsie's knee. She made him recite all his new nursery rhymes and do the hand actions for his Auntie. After a few broken versions of Incey-Wincey Spider, Five Little Ducks and something Elsie had never heard before about a currant bun, Connor happily returned to his crayons and scribbled all over the paper. Jodie talked quickly and Elsie listened slowly, not really wanting to hear how happy Jodie was and how wonderful it would be to be Mrs Graham Rice. Elsie's thoughts were quite the opposite and she tried hard to keep a suitable look in her eyes as she listened to Jodie flutter on with so much energy and happiness. It was shortly before nine when Jodie remembered she had to take Connor to his child minder while she popped into town. Inaccurately, she fumbled to collect the crayons and paper from across the floor where Connor had spread them., then she gathered him up in her arms, plonked him in the buggy and strapped him in. She whisked round to kiss her Aunt, trotted off happily through the door and left Elsie in silence with her thoughts. The quietness of the room was all the more obvious now after the sudden whirlwind of excitement that had just left, taking the noise with it. The ticking of the clock on the bedside table seemed to grow even louder against the silent backdrop and became almost hypnotic. Elsie stared at the clock, watching the second hand click its way round, lost in thought.

By the time Elsie had got to Tom's room, he had finished his breakfast and the pots had been taken away. She didn't smile as she entered the room and Tom noticed straight away that her usual breathing display was somewhat subdued and less noisy.

"What's bit you?" he said flatly.

Elsie told Tom everything. Totally convinced that Graham was up to no good she had to prove it to Jodie without hurting her feelings. She had strong suspicions that Graham had stayed out all night with a female friend but she openly admitted that this was pure speculation on her part. Tom questioned her motives, politely, to make sure that Elsie didn't have a hidden agenda or that she was just against Jodie having someone else in her life that might be as important to her as she was. Tom was good at exploring people. With a subtle blend of psychology and manipulation, he could ask the right kind of question that made people think and reveal themselves. He had been a counsellor once, so he claimed. It was one of his many jobs he had as he was "trying to find out what it was he wanted to be when he grew up," as he put it.

Helen came in for a sit down and a chat. Elsie recited to Helen almost word for word. Tom thought he might be able to lip-sync alongside Elsie but thought better of it, not wanting to belittle her obvious concerns. Helen asked similar questions to those that Tom asked, only with slightly different wording.

"You two ganging up on me?" she questioned, almost jokingly.

"Only trying to listen and help," answered Helen with a smile. She put her hand on Elsie's knee reassuringly.

It took quite a while and a lot of effort to calm Elsie down, but calm her they did. The three of them talked about the concept of marriage and their own experiences. Tom didn't have any marriage experience, but he had lived with a few girlfriends. Elsie loved her husband dearly and was faithful to the end. So faithful in fact that she never had a relationship with any other man since he died, although there were times when she wished she had. Helen was lost to Nathan, she loved him or at least she thought she loved him, but she was a bit cautious around marriage. The more she explained things to Tom and Elsie, the more she questioned herself. She began to doubt what once she was so sure of. Never before had she considered her relationship to be insecure but she came to the discomforting conclusion that she just took it for granted, warts and all. She pondered on the multitude of minor concerns she had about Nathan and created a mental list for herself, trying to balance the audit with a range of pros and cons. Natalie popped by just before lunch to collect Elsie and Helen left with them to make a start on the lunchtime rounds. Natalie escorted Elsie back to her room, talking and laughing all the way down the corridor. They talked about dancing and music. Elsie's music of choice wasn't so different to Natalie's, but the names had changed over the years. Natalie talked about the kind of boys she liked and Elsie told Natalie all about the man downstairs. Natalie chuckled and explained that she could arrange for the two of them to meet if she liked. Elsie quickly refused, waving her hands and laughing. As the sunlight illuminated Elsie's face as her door was opened, Natalie could see her cheeks had blushed red.

* * * * *

He walked freely through the street in the broad daylight. Nobody took much notice of who was doing what during daylight hours and most people in this affluent suburban estate were out at work, so he had no need to fear recognition. As he rounded a cul-de-sac lined with large semi-detached status symbols, he paid particular attention to doors and windows. Down wide drives he could see passed the houses and into some of the gardens. Like a seasoned poacher, he knew all the best forms of hunting; reflections in windows that could see around corners, visible shadows revealing unseen activity. A few houses ahead he noticed a young woman taking clothes off her washing line. He slowed his pace and watched her in the back garden as she worked diligently with her laundry. Satisfied that he found what he was looking for, he stopped and raised his arm, as if looking at the time so he could take a long look without being too obvious and then he quickly scanned the cul-de-sac for other people. Nobody anywhere. That was good.

He saw the young girl disappear into her house, so he walked quickly down the driveway and toward the back garden. Close to the wall, without looking too suspicious, and rounded the corner to the back door with another last look over his shoulder out toward the street. Nobody. Standing very still he waited by the open door, listening. He heard the sound of footsteps running up the stairs and stepped inside. Scanning his environment, he looked around an open door into the living room where he was met by a rather curious dog. It jumped off the couch with a small insignificant bark and bounded over to him, stopping just in front of him with its tail wagging furiously. The black and brown Doberman-cross tilted its head and poked out is tongue as it panted heavily. He stood silent and still for a moment and then, quickasaflash, he kicked out. His foot flew straight and true and connected with the lower jaw of the animal, sending the head up and back with a loud crack. The dog staggered backwards, dazed, lowered its head then fell over onto its side. The dog twitched and whimpered with its broken jaw hanging open and limp against the floor as it bled profusely. He left the room smiling and went back into the hall. The sound of footsteps still paced out above him as he closed the back door quietly. The dog's whimpering faded, although it became high pitched so he pulled the door closed. All quiet. All safe. The phone at the bottom of the stairs started to ring.

"Shit!" he whispered, startled, and quickly looked for a hiding place.

The phone stopped and he heard the muffled sounds of someone speaking coming from upstairs.

"Phew!" he whispered with a laugh.

Concentrating on her voice, he walked through to the foot of the stairs and started up until he reached the landing and saw the door to the room she was in. Cautiously, quietly, he sneaked up to the doorway and waited. The conversation turned to the farewells, and when he was sure his timing was right, he pushed the door wide with both hands.

"Hi honey I'm home!" he shouted at the startled girl as he burst through the door.

The door flew open with such a force that it knocked her onto her back and split her cheek. She was stunned, dazed and confused. He smiled as he fell onto her, like a kestrel dropping like lead from above to snare its prey. As he sat on her chest he covered her mouth with his hand.

"Good girl," he growled.

She was quite small and thin, and she didn't struggle much. Her fear had stolen her strength and she had been shocked into silence. With frightened eyes she stared up at him, locked in the nightmare. Her futile attempts to get free were feeble.

"Is that all you've got?" he sneered as he brought his nose to hers and stared straight into her terrified eyes.

She could smell his skin, his breath as he rested eye to eye with his nose touching hers. He flicked his tongue in and out quickly like a snake sniffing the air, and tasted her lips. She tried to turn away but he held her firm. In inhaled her perfume and quivered in anticipation.

Fragile and useless, she could not even find the strength to scream. Like a cat with a ball of wool, he flipped her over and pulled at her T-shirt. It tore easily and he wrenched it off her to reveal the back of her black lace bra, which he pulled open in an instant. Again he flipped her over and exposed her firm young breasts. He grabbed them hard and squeezed, his nails digging into her skin. She tried to scream, but through the tears and the fear all she could do was choke a feeble gurgle. He laughed deliberately close to her ear. She began to sob helplessly, her reddened breasts, scratched and sore, painful. So young and weak, no match for this man, she surrendered and could do nothing to evade him. When he turned his attention to her skirt, he noticed that she had urinated and she was trembling.

"Filthy fuckin' bitch!" he growled as he slapped her hard across her face.

He felt good. He felt strong. Again and again from the left, from the right, he slapped her face until she stopped crying and her head flopped from side to side with each contact. Her face was bright red and her nose was bleeding. Surprised, he leaned in close to listen to her breath, hovering in silence as he felt her whispered breath on his cheek. Relieved, he sat back a little and removed all of her clothes very carefully. He stood above her and admired her young body. The blood that had smeared across her face had begun to dry. The pale flesh against the red mask aroused him. He unbuttoned his trousers and lowered them around his thighs. Quickly, as if not to miss the moment, he masturbated as he kneeled over her and smiled as he watched his semen spill out across her. He immediately fell onto her unconscious body and like a massage with sensuous oils, smeared his seed into her neck and breasts. After a moment to admire his work, he walked across the hall to the bathroom and wiped his hands and penis on a towel on a rail. He began to fill the wash basin and added a little soap that he found on the windowsill before he returned to the bedroom.

She was still out cold; silent, cold, pale and beautiful with warm red scratches and dried blood; modern art. Lovingly, he stroked her stomach, then across her thigh and down her leg. With a total change of mood, he grabbed her ankle and dragged her out of the room. She bumped loosely off the skirting board in the hallway and the doorframe to the bathroom and he swore at her awkwardness. When he had laid her out in the bathroom, carefully, he bathed her gently as she lay limp and lifeless on the cold tiles. He listened to her breathing again but this time he heard nothing. With great care he dried her and mercilessly carried her back to the bedroom over his shoulder. He clumsily dropped her down onto the bed and apologised to her for doing so. With a smile, he admired her young body as he slowly removed his own clothes.

* * * * *

Helen deliberately served Tom his dinner last so that she could sit with him in his room and talk. She had every intention of telling him how his story had upset her, but whenever she was in a position to do so, she couldn't force the words out of her mouth in the way she had imagined. No sooner had she formed a sentence and plucked up the courage than Tom would start on another rambling and she couldn't get a word in. They both sat with their sandwiches and side-salads and Tom talked about his counselling days as a youth worker. Tom explained to Helen that he used to work with the "difficult kids that nobody else could handle" as he put it and had had a troublesome childhood himself. He explained that he was raised in a broken home … was kicked out as a teenager … homeless for a while … got involved with drink and drugs … "the whole disaffected menu" as he put it. All the things your parents worry about, but not his, so he said, his parents were never concerned enough to wonder where he was or what he was doing. It was because of this rocky start in life that he thought he could help people. He had turned himself around, he explained, and stopped all the drinking and smoking before he got too ill to enjoy the prime of his life. He spoke of his colleagues, the ones he liked in any case, with a great smile across his face. He told of happy outings and the success stories with some of the young people he had worked with. He told of kids that came from chaotic backgrounds with alcoholic parents that had been dragged up on housing estates that resembled war zones. He told how they had changed their own lives with the help of Tom and his colleagues. Tom's voice betrayed his love for the work and his facial expressions lit the joy of his memories. He smiled a lot while he spoke and emphasised the positive aspects of even the most negative of people. Helen frowned as she thought about these obnoxious thugs and how he respected them. She knew she would not have been able to work with the likes of drug addicts and thieves. Impressed by his character, she momentarily forgot that she had something important to discuss with him.

As the sandwiches disappeared and the salad began to look lost and limp on the edge of the plate, his stories turned to the things he didn't like; management, government targets and record keeping. His tone lowered, his brow furrowed and his eyes narrowed as he recalled a colleague he was not so keen on.

"Its not that I hated her," he began, "in fact I might have fancied her under any other circumstances, but she took the piss out of me constantly; I think she thought she was being funny. We worked together a lot. She shouldn't have taken the piss out me. It was terrible, and in front of the young people at the youth centre too. I got so angry with her. I swore I'd sort her out, and after weeks of waiting for an opportunity, I did!" he laughed a single syllable "ha!" as he finished the sentence.

After a short pause he leaned in closer to Helen and said, in a low whispering voice,

"I thought if I sabotaged her car just enough to increase the risk of an accident, then I would be doing nothing more than giving fate a helping hand," he leaned back against his pillows.

"I swapped a couple of pipes you see, good ones for old, manky, rotten ones. I got them from a scrap yard. I thought they would never trace that and put it down to a genuine accident."

He shrugged his shoulders slightly and raised his palms to the ceiling. Helen was worried where this was going and shook her head slightly. She was about to speak but unfortunately she had no words to say and Tom started off again.

"I knew she had to go up to Liverpool at the weekend, something to do with her racing horses, a meeting or competition or something," he fluttered a hand in the air as if shooing away a fly.

"A long, fast drive on the motorway, all the way. I got the old pipes from a scrapyard. Almost by chance actually, I was going over Railway Bridge, overlooking the yard when I saw a car that looked exactly like hers, all smashed up and dented but it was the same, exactly the same colour and everything. I couldn't pass up a chance like that," he laughed a little, "it was a sign, wasn't it?" he nodded.

Helen felt the blood rush out of her face and gather in her stomach. She came over cold and wrapped her arms around her waist. She wanted to leave, though her curiosity and fear wouldn't her.

"I replaced the pipes a couple of days before the weekend she was going. I snook out to the car park and popped the hood. She'd gone on some errand and would be gone for some time. It was easy, really. Nobody around, most of the car park was hidden from view, even from the CCTV. I just took a screwdriver from the toolbox in the store, unscrewed the clips and took the pipes off. They leaked a little, but nothing much, a quick wipe with an old rag and it was all gone. Ruined my shoes though! I screwed the old rotten pipes in place. Bingo!" he raised his palms as he shrugged again.

"Just for good measure, I loosened a few bolts here and there and banged a few metal pipes out of shape. It was that simple, even with my limited knowledge of cars and engines! I mean, I didn't know what I was doing – I only wanted to make things dangerous, but then they turned out much better than that!"

Helen gasped slightly and covered her mouth with her hand, suddenly feeling nauseous.

"She was almost there on Saturday morning, according to the news, when her engine burst into flames! Apparently, she braked hard and the horsebox rammed into the back of her. It was a terrible mess. I saw the pictures on TV. They had to shoot one of the horses on site, but the other escaped without injury, quite miraculous I suppose. I was glad for it though; I didn't want to hurt the horses. Other cars and lorries piled into the back and the whole thing got very messy."

He snuggled himself down into his pillows and turned away from Helen, closed his eyes and smacked his lips. Helen could feel the pressure building up in her ears, like she was under water. She leaned forward, rested her elbows on her knees and clasped her hands in front of her, as her eyes grew damp.

"She was badly burned with multiple injuries and died some days later in hospital. She never regained consciousness, apparently. I was right about them thinking there were no suspicious circumstances though."

He fell silent, snuggled his head a little more and released a long, low sigh before gently closing his eyes. Helen was getting colder, her arms and legs seemed weightless. She sat for a moment or two and contemplated what she had heard. Her mouth was still slightly open so she raised a hand to cover it as she got up and turned to leave.

She walked out into the corridor leaving the shocking story behind her in the room. The echoes of what she had just heard played on in her ears. Silently and slowly she walked to the entrance hall, zombie like, unresponsive to the farewell gestures from her colleagues. She went into the staff room to collect her coat and scarf from her locker. It was as if she had switched her body on to autopilot; she was not thinking of what she was doing but just doing it as she had done it countless times. She drove home in silence, battling with the thoughts of what she had been told. They tossed around in her head like a rough sea, crashing onto the rocks of some desolate uninhabited island. Her autopilot had managed to get her home safely despite her consciousness not concentrating but reluctantly surrendering to the merciless torrent of chaotic thought. She pushed open the heavy wooden door to her house, picked up the paper off the doormat and took off her coat and scarf. She walked through to the kitchen and tossed the paper on the coffee table as she passed through the sitting room into the kitchen. Still unthinking and purely reacting, she pulled off her shoes, threw them lightly into the corner and went over to the fridge. In silence, she made herself a cup of tea and went through to the lounge to sit in her favourite spot, feet tucked up to her bum, knees over to the left, holding her hot cup of tea in both hands. The thoughts still tumbled around while she sipped. For an hour she sat in silence until the evening grew dim. Suddenly, front door opened and disturbed the stillness.

"Hello? You home?" Nathan called.

"Yes, I got off a bit early," she replied quietly as she stared blankly into the middle-distance.

She felt the warmth slowly coming back to her, knowing that she was no longer alone.

"That's good. Fancy going out for dinner?"

He pecked her on the cheek as he passed, unfolded the paper as he took a seat beside her and stretched out his legs on the coffee table.

"Not yet. Maybe later."

Helen snapped out of her trance, finished her cold tea and leaned forward to put the empty cup on the table in front of her. She backhanded his feet slightly and stated "Off!" in a very stern voice. Instantly, he dropped his feet to the floor with a smile.

"This is terrible," he said, shaking his head, "a major pile-up just outside of Leicester. Three dead and four critical. Some poor woman's car burnt up on the motorway and caused a right mess. Look at that!"

He handed the open paper with a large colour photograph to Helen, as he got up to switch the TV on. She couldn't believe what she was reading.

"Tom told me a story like this today, just before I left," she said in disbelief, "he said he sabotaged some girl's car on her way to Liverpool and she died after being in a pile up."

Her voice trailed away as she fixed her focus on the television. There were pictures of the crash site as a journalist relayed the story from the roadside, trying her best to display genuine concern for the families of the dead and injured. There was a burned out car smashed beyond recognition, three other vehicles in various states of damage, and numerous shards of debris strewn across the carriageway. Blue lights flashed off every reflective surface. The evening was growing dark which emphasised the horror of the crash site. Helen told Nathan about the story Tom had told her while her eyes were fixed on the News all the time.

"You didn't take him seriously did you? He's a mixed-up old man, Helen. He's getting old and needs to talk. Obviously read the papers and then got carried away in his imagination. Don't worry about it."

He put his hand on her shoulder and sat down beside her again. She was obviously distressed but Nathan had not looked her in the eye since he got home and hadn't noticed. Helen, however, was all too aware of the total lack of eye contact and had added it her mental list of doubts about her relationship.

"Let's go to dinner, I'm starving and can't be bothered to cook or wash pots."

"OK," she surrendered, "I suppose you're right. Maybe senile dementia is kicking in," she tried hard to stop her thoughts, "he's just mixed up," she smiled a very fake smile as she got up.

She wasn't totally convinced that Tom was mixed up at all but she was trying to think herself into believing it. The way he had told the story was too firm, too realistic. Still worrying, she slowly went up the narrow stairs to get ready. Nathan managed to book a table at the fourth restaurant he tried and then phoned for a cab, before he skipped up the stairs to join Helen. He stopped outside the bedroom door and watched her from the hallway. In the mirror through the slightly open door he could see her getting undressed as she stripped down to her white lace panties and matching bra. He became aroused and in his excitement and leaned forward to get a better view. Helen noticed the door twitch in the mirror; she turned and smiled. She beckoned him seductively into the bedroom, and began to lower her knickers, slowly wriggling her hips. As Nathan walked slowly into the room, unbuttoning his shirt and making eye contact for the first time, she threw a pair of trousers at him. She was not in the mood for any intimacy right now, though he would not understand how distracted she really was.

"Just get dressed, love, we don't want to be late!"

The restaurant was not busy, but there were a few couples here and there. Nathan thought it odd that so many tables were empty on a Saturday night and hoped he had not chosen a poor quality restaurant that everybody knew about except him. The initial concern was quickly exacerbated by another mild anxiety suggesting that this restaurant might turn out to be a bit more expensive than he had hoped. The other customers ate quietly and sipped their wine as they talked about work and family. Helen and Nathan were greeted by the maitre d' in a smart black tuxedo and shown over to a table by a window with a candle and a rose on it. Nathan looked at the presentation and commented on how it got in the way but Helen thought it rather sweet. Nathan complained that the tables were never quite big enough in these places as he rearranged the condiments and table dressings. Helen resigned herself to his total lack of romance and simply made herself comfortable, tilting her head at Nathan. She scanned the other diners, paying particular attention to the other women and the clothes they were wearing. She looked at shoes and handbags and rated them on her own personal scale, either loving them, liking them or not. One of the men on the table across the room looked familiar to Helen, but she couldn't place him. She stared at him, trying to think. When he made eye contact with her she smiled and waved discreetly hoping that he would recognise her and not think her rude for staring. He smiled nervously and nodded in her direction before pulling in his chair and turning to face his beautiful company. Then she noticed that his beautiful company was Lucy; a colleague of hers. Helen hardly ever worked with Lucy directly because they were on different shifts but they did know each other a little from training courses and crossover times at either end of their working hours. Lucy waved and smiled and Helen returned the gesture. To Helen's surprise, Nathan waved back too, but she didn't question him. Instead, she added another mental note to her ever-expanding list of doubts. The waiter delivered the menus with a quiet welcome and Nathan promptly began reading aloud all the French words he couldn't pronounce and complained about the simplest dishes being made to appear complicated so they could demand a higher price. After much deliberation, they ordered their meals and turned to face each other.

Helen wanted to talk about both of the traffic incidents over dinner. She explained Tom's story and the way he had arranged the accident to happen. Nathan tried his best to change the subject, trying to tell her not to worry; he was just muddled up between the newspaper and real life. He insisted that "It was not that easy. You can't just change a fuel pipe like that!" and how improbable the whole story was. He tried, and he tried again. When his tone became slightly angry, she stopped and asked him about his day. Helen bumped into Lucy in the Ladies between courses and said a quick hello while washing her hands and adjusting her hair in the mirror. Lucy explained that she was out on a first date and it was going really well. They had met at work just recently. She spoke about his nice eyes and sense of humour, although she never mentioned his name. She was so excited and keen to get back to her new friend that she did not stay long enough for an in-depth conversation, which disappointed Helen; she would have liked the distraction of all the details. When she got back to the table, Nathan was pouring more wine. They sat together until they were the last two in the restaurant and the candles had melted away. It was only when the maitre d' gave a gentle "ah-hem" from a polite distance that they decided it was time to leave. Nathan left a healthy tip in the little brass plate by the till and took a handful of complimentary mints from the finger bowl while the waiter's attention was turned. He popped one in his mouth straight away and dropped the rest in his jacket pocket. Helen shook her head and rolled her eyes. Why he ever needed to take more than one or two was beyond her. She knew she would be putting the rest of them in the bin on laundry day when she emptied his pockets.

They trotted off into the night together. They laughed and joked down the street to the taxi rank and were home within the hour. Helen remarked how nights like this reminded her of when they first started going out. Her cheeks had become rosy from too much wine and a lot of smiling. She reminded herself that she did love him after all, although she quickly concluded that it was easier to love him after too much wine. Nathan chased Helen through the house, up the stairs and into bed. The sheets were cold at first but soon warmed up. It was getting light by the time they cuddled up to go to sleep. Helen curled up with her cheek on Nathan's chest and his arm around her as he held her shoulder. Just as they were nodding off, the radio came on with the six-o-clock news. Helen banged her face into her pillow several times with a muffled scream before she turned on her back, kicked off the duvet and made her way to the shower with loud, deliberate footsteps. Nathan groaned and hid his head under his pillow.

She flicked on the television as she passed through the living room into the kitchen, rubbing her wet hair with the towel as she walked. The familiar music of the news faded in and then out again. She came back into the room with a cup of tea, the towel draped around her neck, her dressing gown tied tightly around her middle and tufts of cotton wool between her toes.

The newsreader was recapping the car incident of yesterday. Something was out of place for Helen. Startled by the spark of a memory, she quickly put her tea down on the table, missed the coaster and splashed a little over the remote control. She reached toward the shelf under the table for yesterdays' paper. With her mouth half open in anticipation, she flicked through the pages, found the story and read through the lines as quickly as she could. She dropped the paper in her lap, her mouth still open, only now in disbelief. There was no mention of any horses involved in yesterday's incident.

SUNDAY

Nathan lay motionless in bed with his hands clasped behind his neck as he listened to the distant sound of church bells harmonised with the birdsong from deep within the trees outside. Having no reason or inclination to hurry, he waited for the bells to finish tolling and breathed in deeply and slowly. He rolled himself round and out of bed, scratched his hair and wiped his face with his hands. He paused and sniffed suddenly at his palms with a curled down mouth and furrowed his forehead. He looked at his hands, puzzled, and walked through to the bathroom. He pulled open the mirrored cabinet and saw his reflection flip quickly off to one side, which made him flinch as the bright window reflected in his eyes as the door passed his face. He reached in for his shaving foam, paused and then changed his mind. He rubbed his chin and shook his head.

"Don't think I'll bother with that for another day or so," he whispered to himself.

He washed his face straight from the tap, sending splashes of water all across the floor and down the tiled wall. As if working against the clock, he brushed his teeth quickly, spraying white flecks of foamed toothpaste across the mirror, which he half-heartedly wiped into a dragged-out smear. He dried himself on the towel from the rack and threw it over the side of the bath, where it slid down slowly at first then gathered momentum into a crumpled heap at the tap end. He looked at his reflection again, ruffled his hair with his hand, blew himself a kiss and then returned to the bedroom. He pulled on a pair of jeans and a loose shirt before he skipped off downstairs. The television played out a decorating programme to an empty room; Helen must have left it on when she went to work. After he wiped the tea from the remote on his jeans, he changed the channel, and then went through to the kitchen to make himself a cup of coffee. To his surprise, he found a box of cereal in the fridge.

"Were you awake this morning, Helen?" he tutted.

He put the cereal back in the cupboard and retrieved the coffee from the next shelf. The kettle was still warm and didn't take long to boil. He tossed the spoon towards the sink, which thudded against the bowl and bounced noisily over the draining board. Back in the room, he sipped his drink and saw the newspaper on the couch, still open at the main story. He looked left and right, as if crossing the road, and then put his feet up on the table with a smile, sipped his coffee and watched the news. There had been several incidents of young women being followed by a stranger after dark over the past few nights. Some had been attacked in broad daylight, others in their own homes. The frequency of attacks had been increasing over the last few weeks and the police had confirmed that a serial attacker was at large. One young woman had been raped after the Crawler, as the media were calling him, had appeared in her bedroom while she slept. She had been tied to the bed and violently raped repeatedly. There was no sign of a break in. Her partner had found her unconscious in the early hours of the morning and called the police. She confirmed that the doors and windows were locked when she returned home with no sign of any break in or struggle. She told the police in her statement that everything was 'perfectly normal' until she found her girlfriend in the bedroom. The photographs of her facial injuries were shocking, though Nathan just stared, transfixed, almost impressed. Nobody had noticed anybody in the area that night although the police described a young man, of medium build with dark hair and dark eyes based on previous witness' accounts of the Crawler. He had a local accent and wore black clothes. The photo fit was of a man wearing a black balaclava and revealed only a pair of piercing eyes.

"Well that narrows it down then!" he stated sarcastically as he put his mug on the table.

Police warned women to be vigilant and keep their windows and doors locked after dark. This man was a serious threat and his crimes were increasing in severity. Nathan leaned forward and listened to the story with interest, a smile grew on his lips and he shook his head.

"CCTV on every bloody street corner and they saw nothing! What a bunch of losers!" he laughed as he flicked the television off.

He slipped into a pair of soft leather shoes, scooped his car keys and mobile phone out of a bowl on the sideboard and left the house, smiling to himself. As he sat in his car, he flipped open his phone and scrolled through the menu to 'Sunday Lunch'. He pressed the little green phone and put the mobile to his ear as he began to reverse down the driveway into the lifeless street.

* * * * *

Helen had taken her morning quite slowly, not really concentrating on her work. Her mind was full of thoughts about Tom and the story of the sabotaged car. She wasn't looking forward to seeing him this morning and was a little apprehensive about going into his room. She paused outside, with the palm of her hand hovering parallel to the door; her head bowed and eyes closed. She took a deep breath, lifted her chin and knocked four times with her knuckle. She forced a smile before she pushed the door gently open.

"Morning Tom," she faked, "how are you today?"

He was sat up on his pillows, staring at the light and shadow captured in the creases in his bed linen, eyes glazed, as if he were looking at something only he could see. He seemed to be washed with a wave of calmness.

"I dream, Helen," he said slowly "of things gone by."

He paused, slowly blinking as if his eyelids were heavy.

"Are you in love Helen, truly in love?" he turned to look at her.

Helen didn't know what to say. She wanted to say "Yes" instantly, but the list she had compiled in her mind over the past few days was getting too long to ignore. She doubted the truth in her chosen response. She flustered and shook her head, shrugged her shoulders and opened and closed her mouth a few times. He didn't give her a chance to reply, he just smiled lazily and seemed to be drifting, half asleep. Thoughts of medication flooded Helen's mind; had he taken something to make him this drowsy?

"I met my first love in the Tiffany Caverns," he began thoughtfully, "when I was a young teenager. Lust really I suppose, but what's the difference when you're a teenager?" he spoke slowly, as if he was tired and on the edge of sleep.

"There was a disco every Saturday afternoon for the under 18s. It was a dive of a place really, with a round dance floor, too many bright lights and a row of dark alcoves down one side. Private little caves with a table and chairs in. They even had plastic palm trees and rocks around the place in a vain attempt to make it look tropical!"

He smiled and seemed to be waking up, like a patient recovering from anaesthesia, his energy increased slowly. Helen felt weak so she sat on the end of his bed but then remembered that it was against company policy so she reluctantly swapped herself over to the unwelcoming chair.

"She was standing on the edge of the dance floor, swaying slightly while watching her friends dancing to some awful pop rubbish. She saw me and smiled, I smiled back. Wherever she went I followed, watching her sexy little arse sway very nicely under her tight little skirt. I fell in love with her hair first. It was long, blonde and curly. She smelled good too; I noticed that when I got up close behind her. We talked for a while at the bar and I eventually persuaded her into one of the alcoves. She was a good kisser; I just dreamed that kiss all over again. We got very friendly in that alcove! She must have been ready for it herself because she unzipped my trousers."

He almost chuckled as he spoke. His eyes were closed and his hands hovered in front of him as if twitching at the strings of two marionettes.

"I reached round and pulled up her skirt and do you know what I found?" he raised his index finger out in front him and cocked his head to one side, "Stockings!"

He raised both hands with palms upward in front of him before letting them fall back down by his sides.

"I was in heaven! We played with each other for ages in that alcove. She was so wet by the time I'd cum. I remember that feeling very well. I felt all light-headed and giddy. My legs wouldn't work properly!" he giggled.

"She was breathing heavily, like she'd been running. I remember so clearly, I pretended to wipe my face so I could smell my fingers! We cleaned ourselves up and eventually got another drink. She had to wipe some of my muck off the table and we laughed about it."

He sat back and relaxed, his eyes seemed to droop. Helen dipped her chin and raised her eyebrows; she was shocked. Why after all this time had he opened up like this? It was so out of character for this kind and gentle old man. Helen could not decide if he had begun to lose his mind or if he really had experienced these things as a young man. She knew it was hard to imagine elderly people having a youth, but then he must have had some kind of life.

"When we left, I walked her home. The streetlights had come on by then. It must have been autumn because it was only four o'clock or thereabouts. I always got a bit morose in autumn."

He shut his eyes and slouched over to one side.

"I kissed her outside her front door. She didn't invite me in. She said her folks were out and she wasn't supposed to have anyone in when she was on her own. Very respectable I suppose. I kissed her again and left."

He turned his head to the other side with his eyes still shut. Helen looked at her watch on her lapel. As she began to adjust her apron and get out of the chair, he murmured and shuffled slightly in his bed. He spoke with a slightly darker tone.

"I wasn't satisfied though."

Helen sat herself back in the chair and listened on, not really wanting to but she felt an irresistible urge to stay, like a frightened teenager watching something scary from behind a cushion. She tried to convince herself that this was a story, and probably never happened.

"I waited until she had gone in and then quietly crept up to the door. I peered through the letterbox and watched her sexy little arse disappear into the kitchen at the end of the hall. I pushed down the handle, real slow, and pushed the door gently. It opened surprisingly quietly. I closed it very carefully behind me, making no noise at all. My heart was pounding; I've never felt more alive!"

He took a deep breath and sighed aloud. With a low, rasping whisper, almost as if he didn't want the girl to hear him, he continued,

"I crept very quietly into the house. I could see her reflection in the kitchen window from the hallway. I crept up to the open door and squeezed myself up against the wall in a tight corner. She came out of the kitchen and right passed me. She turned at the bottom of the stairs; my heart was in my mouth and I shrunk myself right into the corner against the wall and the side of the stairs. She hadn't seen me in the shadows with the fading light."

His whispering grew in volume. Helen leaned forward with her mouth slightly open. She was aware of the stories in the paper and that Tom was an avid reader of the local rag.

"She went upstairs, eating a sandwich and humming to herself. When she was out of sight, I followed her, very quietly, very slowly. I looked through the banister across the floor upstairs and saw the light under one of the doors. She hadn't quite closed it properly. I went over to the door. My heart was pounding so loud I thought she might have heard it and known I was there. I was shaking inside and my hands were sweating. I listened at the door. She was singing to herself. I tried to look through the tiny gap she had left in the doorway but I couldn't see her. I gently pushed the door and it started to open, so slowly it hardly moved at all. With a wider gap I could see her in her mirror. She was getting undressed. She pulled off her top, and then rolled down her stockings. Oh, my excitement was rising; I was so horny I came in my pants there and then."

He opened his eyes and stared into space with an almost wild look on his face.

"I turned and ran as fast as I could, I smashed an ornament off the window sill on top of the stairs and didn't even shut the front door behind me. I ran down the street and all the way home. I've never run as fast in my life!"

He closed his eyes again.

"I enjoyed it though. I enjoyed it very much."

Tom became still. He had his eyes closed with a relaxed, peaceful look on his face. Helen was surprised. She didn't know what to say. She sat for a moment in silence and then began to pull herself up out of the chair. He seemed to have fallen asleep, so as a habit she straightened the bed linen around him. She noticed that he was erect under the thin bed sheets. Helen stared at him in disbelief with her mouth slightly open. Thoughts raced through her head again. She felt the room moving slightly as if she were in a lift. Her ears began to pound in time with her accelerating heartbeat. She dropped herself into the chair, put her head in her hands and breathed deeply for a moment or two until the wave faded away.

* * * * *

Natalie knocked politely on Elsie's door and pushed it wide as she walked in with her tray of breakfast cereal. She was about to say her good mornings when she noticed that Elsie was not in her room. She placed the tray on the table and looked through to the bathroom. There was water on the floor, the towel on the end of the bed was damp and the mirror was still steamed around the edges but Elsie was nowhere to be seen. Natalie turned to leave and noticed that her bionic chair was down in the seated position and the grabbing device was missing from its usual peg. With a sharp intake of breath, she put her hand over her mouth and reached out to lean against the wall. She stood momentarily motionless, open-mouthed before she ran out of the room, along the corridor, down the stairs two at a time and into the reception area.

"Elsie isn't in her room! Has she got any appointments this morning? Where's the logbook? Has she been past this way?" Natalie asked, speaking so quickly she almost tripped over her own words.

"No appointments on a Sunday, Nat, why?" replied the young redhead on reception, straightening the paperwork Natalie was busy ruffling on the desk.

"Oh there's something very wrong, very wrong," shook Natalie, covering her mouth again "Elsie is not in her room and her chair is down!"

"Her chair is down? What do you mean her chair is down? Natalie you make no sense. Slow down and tell me all about it," she shook her head, frowned, and took hold of Natalie by the shoulders in an attempt to keep her still.

"Her chair is never down," explained Natalie, "when she wants to sit in her chair, its up, then she lowers it. When she gets out of her chair, it rises and stays up till she gets in it again."

"OK, Nat. We'll make a few phone calls. She has a niece doesn't she?" the receptionist turned to the filing cabinet behind her and pulled open a drawer, "perhaps they've gone out for the day."

"Get the police," stated Natalie, very matter-of-fact, "get the police NOW because something is very wrong!"

* * * * *

Helen sat in a large office, with fully laden bookshelves across the longest wall and a large wooden table with an inlaid leather top in front of the window. There was a computer on the desk that looked very out of place in this dark wood and leather environment, and a selection of stationery items. The chair she was in was very ornate with carved wooden arms and legs with studded leather cushions on the back and the seat. Helen stroked the carved animal heads on the ends of the arms as she admired the grandeur of the room. It all looked very majestic under the watchful eye of St Anthony, painted onto a huge free hanging canvas on the wall to her left. He was standing on a hillside with his arms outstretched. He had a child under one arm and an old woman under the other. The child was playing with a lamb while the elderly woman was holding what looked like a piece of cloth or a garment of some kind. St Anthony's golden halo radiated from him in concentric circles, weaving in and out of the clouds and the rainbow behind him in the distance. Helen was lost in the painting, trying to make some sense of all the thoughts in her head when the door clicked open.

"Sorry Helen, I couldn't get away," said the woman's voice behind her.

A slender woman in a smart grey suit and black rimmed spectacles came into view and sat herself down behind the big table. She rearranged the stationery and straightened her jacket.

"That's OK, Lynn, It's been nice to sit in silence and think a bit first."

Helen shuffled in her seat. She couldn't help but notice the large flowery cerise bow around her collar and made a conscious effort to talk to Lynn and not the bow.

"So what's been bothering you? What can I help you with?" asked Lynn, sitting unnaturally upright in her seat, her fingers interlocked on the table in front of her.

Helen took a deep breath and began by telling her supervisor all about Tom and the stories he had told her. Lynn just listened until Helen had poured out the stories, nodding occasionally and making 'hmm' sounds. Eventually, Helen came to a pause; feeling slightly relieved having released the burden. She looked expectantly at Lynn, who had also paused and appeared to be lost in thought. After a fleeting moment in silence which seemed slightly too long for Helen trying not to stare at the bow, Lynn leaned forward and asked,

"You have told me what you have heard, but how do you feel about these stories?"

Helen sat back in her seat with another sigh and began by explaining her relationship with Tom. She explained that Tom had been a crutch for her to lean on and a pillow into which she could cry. She told Lynn that she respected him and that he was quite an ordinary sort of man with nothing untoward about him. He had helped her with her problems, provided her with a second opinion, had been a mirror into which she could pour her concerns and have them paraphrased back at her for her own assessment. Now he was telling her that he has been involved with the death of two women and a serious stalking incident.

"But how do you *feel* about it?" Lynn emphasised, as if the facts of which Helen spoke where irrelevant without any emotional content.

Helen began to sob gently as she explained that she felt scared and confused. She questioned herself as to whether she believed Tom had told these stories after hearing the news and it was nothing more than his mind playing tricks. But then, on the other hand, his stories were only similar to the ones on the news. Had he been adding to them from his imagination? Had he recited the stories from the news as he remembered them, with his imagination filling out the extra details? She puzzled along with Lynn, exploring the ins and outs of the stories, comparing them to the recent events. When all of the facts and feelings had been explored and taken apart, Lynn leaned forward over her desk.

"It is my opinion," started Lynn in a very matter-of-fact tone, "that these stories are Tom's way of adding excitement to his life, especially since he is becoming aware of his life coming to an end. The realisation of death can have a very strange effect on some people, especially if they are scared. He hears these stories in the news and wanders off into a kind of daydream, reliving them in his own context. It is not uncommon for innocent people to confess to crimes they haven't done. It's a kind of attention seeking behaviour, wanting to be noticed, to be famous for something shocking. Sometimes people confess to things that they haven't done in order to release some inner-feelings of guilt."

Lynn looked up to the ceiling in an almost patronising manner and Helen's gaze drifted onto her bow.

"Hypothetically speaking, it could be possible that Tom has committed some kind of personal sin in the past that he feels guilty for and so he confesses to the current situations in order to express and be punished for that latent guilt."

Lynn paused and looked straight at Helen, who was just staring blankly forward, not totally convinced by what she was hearing.

"If you are unsure, you can check the stories out," offered Lynn, "he says that both of the serious incidents were in the paper at the time didn't he? So that's were you start. The library on Maine Square has an extensive collection of media files on disc. Do a bit of research and read the events of the time. Do you know which year to look for?"

Lynn jotted down notes on a pad as she spoke.

"No. Tom doesn't know how old he is."

After a silent pause, Helen laughed. It suddenly sounded funny. The seriousness was ridiculed in an instant. The single line lifted the weight from her shoulders, like she had taken off her heavy rucksack and come to rest in a pleasant meadow after trudging for miles over wild country.

"You see? Now that might put some perspective on things," explained Lynn, leaning back, "If you are still unsure and want to settle your thoughts, look it up in his records, do a bit of digging."

Lynn smiled and removed her spectacles. She held them up by the arm and waved them round in a small circle like some sort of victory flag.

"OK" Helen replied, nodding, as she rose out of her chair, straightening her skirt.

Lynn said her goodbyes as she placed her spectacles on the desk and took up her notes. Helen thought her manner returned unnaturally quickly to being cold and clinical after showing so much concern only a few moments ago. It was a trick Helen envied; how could she learn to control her emotions so well? She turned to leave and had a last look over to the large canvas. St Anthony was staring at her with the faintest of smiles and she noticed the child was crying. Helen paused outside the office as the heavy door shut slowly behind her. The dull thud was enough to make her move onward down the corridor and back to the main office behind reception.

She pulled open the filing cabinets and scanned the labels for Tom's file. She pulled it out and sat herself at the desk by the window, flicked through various sheets of paper and quickly examined the information, panned out the pages on the desk and cross-referenced the details. She picked up the Initial Referral Form with Tom's details on it. Tom would be 97 on Tuesday. He had two previous addresses in the five years before he joined the Home eight years ago. Helen scanned the information and made notes. She wrote down his full name, his date of birth and his previous address, folded the paper into her pocket and got up to leave. She just got to the door when she realised she had left everything out on the desk so she turned back and scooped up the pages randomly into the file. Unlike her usual organised self, she dropped the file into the cabinet, out of place, and left the room quickly.

When Helen arrived at the Library she made enquiries at the main desk. An enthusiastic librarian escorted Helen to the media section and showed her where the files were stored. He explained that all digital media coverage was not available to take out so she should print whatever she needs on the printer in the room with the viewers. He was young and stood slightly too close for Helen's liking. When he was sure she understood what she was doing and how to retrieve the information from the discs, he took a step back and pulled a chair out for Helen to sit on. He scribbled something on a piece of paper and then handed it to Helen.

"My mobile," he said quietly, tapping the piece of paper with his index finger, "direct line to me and as much fun as you can handle, whenever you want it."

He smiled and walked away backwards; nodding and grinning like a mischievous schoolboy. Helen just shook her head and scrumpled up the piece of paper. She put it on the table, beside the media viewer and then flicked it into the bookshelf opposite, where it vanished off behind a copy of 'Media Studies: The Essential Aspects'. She loaded up the first disc and found it easy to navigate through the information. The stories and photographs looked old, although things hadn't changed in the way that she had imagined. It seemed to be that people had always done the same things but only with different technology. She almost forgot what she looking for and became entranced by the history. After a little research and half a page of scribbled lines, she changed the discs. She continued searching through the local newspapers until she came across a small story about a 'Garden Creeper'.

Apparently, a young man had been seen going through gardens and looking into people's houses. It was assumed he was a burglar checking out the property but nothing was ever taken and there were no break-ins in that area. The following week, the story surfaced again, this time in more detail as a young woman had been sexually assaulted in her own garden. Two days later, the Garden Creeper had made the headlines with a violent rape in a young woman's house. All in all, there were 19 sexual assaults and seven rapes. The Garden Creeper had only ever appeared to be active between October and January, with no mention of him during the summer months. Helen was shocked by what she was reading. She scribbled down notes and printed out sections of the papers. She trawled through the digital archives and pulled out the national papers. She scanned through and searched for the Garden Creeper and sure enough she found him. The police had never charged anyone with the crime although they did have DNA and witness statements. The investigation had been high profile since the first rape and the police had been under public scrutiny as the papers had swirled up their usual media storm over the whole case. Helen checked to the end of the disc but could find no further mention of him. Police assumed that he had either gone to prison for something else or, more likely, that he had left the country. The file had been left open.

Helen slumped back in the chair. The stories read like the script of an over-blown soap. She ran her fingers through her hair and let out a deep breath before changing the disc and starting again.

"How's it going?" said the smug voice of the young librarian behind her, leaning in too close with his chin almost on her shoulder. He had obviously applied a fresh spray of deodorant and the fragrance was almost overpowering.

"Fine thanks," she said. "Would it be OK to use my mobile in here? I've got to ring my husband and tell him I'll be late home."

She held up her mobile and smiled at the librarian.

"Sorry," was all he said as he turned and walked away.

Helen dropped the mobile phone into her pocket and then clicked open another file to start a new search. The printer on the table to her left was humming as it reeled out page after page of Garden Creeper stories. Helen decided to see if she could find anything to support the story about the mother of Tom's child. She found several deaths associated with drug overdoses and was shocked to think that there were so many in such a small, relatively affluent town. She cross-referenced the ages of the women after she had worked out how old Tom would have been at the time and guessed that the woman would be a year or two either way. After a couple of hours reading, she had found a likely candidate.

Amanda Wilkinson had died of heart failure following a drug overdose at the age of 33. She had been found by a local young man who had been in care and alleged to be searching for his real mother, who he believed to be Amanda, though the police were not at liberty to confirm this, or his identity, to the newspapers. Helen was getting scared. Tom's history seemed somewhat more real, and more sinister, than she had hoped. She collated the printed sheets and her notes and put them in a neat pile next to her. She paused as she thought long and hard about her next action. Knowing that she must, but reluctant to go ahead, she clicked on the icon and started one more search. What she found shocked her and a sinister chill crept over her flesh making all of her tiny hairs stand on end.

She looked at the photographs of carnage on the motorway just south of Liverpool and was almost too scared to read the details. She raised her hands to her mouth as she forced herself through the headline and into the story. The woman driver had suffered life-threatening burns and died in hospital later that week. A horse had been shot at the side of the road, much to the distress of the survivors who actually took time to complain to the authorities. Another had been seen bolting out across the carriageway and over the fields where it was later captured, unharmed. Helen read through damp eyes as lonely tears escaped in single file and slowly trickled down her cheeks. She stared at the monitor in silence, motionless, reading the worst thing she had ever read in her life. She could hear

Tom's voice in her head reading the story to her, every word sharp and tormenting. She reached out quickly, as if the monitor would bite her hand if she were too slow, to flick the switch to 'off' and then sat in silence staring into the lost, fragile eyes of her own reflection in the black monitor screen. The pictures of the mangled wreckage stayed in her mind as she walked solemnly through the library to the brighter world outside.

It was still etched in her memory while she was driving home. She heard the screech of brakes and the whinnies of the horses, the impact of heavy metal and the grinding sounds of the disaster as she showered at home. In the warmth of the comforting water flowing through her hair and over her face, her tears were well hidden. She washed slowly and then slower until she stopped. She leaned back against the wall behind her and slumped slowly down the tiles into the cubicle until she sat against the wall with her arms wrapped around her knees up in front of her. The warm water washed away the tears but not the fear or the confusion.

* * * * *

"She hasn't got any appointments and she isn't in the Health Unit. We've been around her friends rooms and she isn't visiting anyone in the Home either," stated the redhead, looking down at her notes.

"Thank you, Miss…?" replied the constable.

"Ascot, Marie Ascot."

"Thank you Miss Ascot," he said as he jotted down notes in his little black book, "Do you have any surveillance in the building? CCTV? Security Monitoring?"

"No, only CCTV outside the building. There's nothing inside, the only security systems in here are the alarm strips along the wall and the personal alarms in the residents' rooms."

She pointed out the metallic strip running just beneath the Daido. Natalie sobbed quietly into numerous scented tissues that she pulled from a floral box on the desk. The constable asked the receptionist 'some routine questions' in an inquisitive tone. There was no sign of a struggle or a break in and the only cause for concern seemed to be Elsie's beloved bionic chair. From the initial investigation, PC Davis concluded that she probably had not left the grounds and advised the receptionist to inform the managers that all available staff should search the building. She may have tripped or fallen and be trapped somewhere, possibly unconscious. The dangers appeared obvious to the constable and he had difficulty understanding why the staff had not reached the same conclusion.

Natalie sobbed louder,

"She's gone against her will!" she insisted, her tone almost monosyllabic,

"She's been forced out of her chair. She couldn't get out without it lifting her up so somebody else would have to help her! When she gets out of that chair herself, she leaves it up so she can get back into it easier," she continued.

"And we have started searching the building already," added the receptionist, raising an arm around Natalie's shoulders.

The constable turned away from the two women and walked a couple of paces before speaking softly into his radio. There were a few minutes of whisperings, interspersed with crackles and hisses as he discussed the situation with the radio controller. Just as he finished the conversation and turned back to the two, a stout man with a beard appeared at the door holding a walking frame.

"I found this in the basement. It's not one of ours, this one!" he stated, putting the frame on the floor in the middle of the group.

Natalie's sobbing exploded into full on crying and she buried her face in Marie's shoulder. Marie quickly circled her arms around her.

"Its Elsie's," she blubbered, "She never goes anywhere without it. She *can't* go anywhere without it!"

The constable turned to the stout man who introduced himself as Mick. He explained that he worked in the maintenance team and part of his job was to fix and adjust the walking frames and wheelchairs, among other things. The frames were left in the basement for him to collect and work on periodically throughout the week.

"This one turned up in the wrong place at the wrong time and it's a different make to the company issued frames," he stated matter-of-factly.

The constable requested that nobody touch the frame and asked who else worked in the maintenance section. Mick gave a further two names and the constable wrote them in his book. Another crackled conversation took place over the radio and Mick was free to go but was advised that he must make himself available for further questioning later. He assured the constable he was staying at the Home all day to help with the search and would be there whenever anybody needed assistance. He raised his index finger to his forehead and flicked out a small salute as he turned and left the group. Marie and Natalie had gone into the office behind reception. Natalie sat on the sofa and Marie made coffee. The constable came in to join them as he flipped his little black book closed and returned it to his breast pocket. He reached for his radio and turned the volume down.

"I'll stay here and search the basement area with the maintenance team. I've got a WPC coming along shortly and she'll be taking statements from both of you. Is there anybody else in the building that works with Elsie that we should know about?"

"Only her Doctor, Doctor Levy, but she's on annual leave until a week on Monday. There might be a nurse in the Health Unit that could help but you would have to ask them at their office," Marie replied as she handed a coffee to Natalie.

"Their office is down the corridor to the left, there's a green cross on the door, you can't miss it."

The constable thanked the two women and turned to go. Marie sat with Natalie and wrapped an arm around her shoulders as she whispered reassurances that Natalie didn't believe.

* * * * *

The incident room was a busy place, full of police officers coming and going. Criminals were being dragged in and out of side rooms and young offenders waited with their families on a row of miss-matched chairs against the wall. Helen was sat next to a particularly pungent young man who insisted on growling up phlegm in his throat and snorting loudly every few minutes. The woman to her right was sat back in her chair with her arms and legs crossed, her larger frame spilled out across the chairs next to her and invaded Helen's comfort zone. Helen tried to breathe slightly slower than normal in an attempt to inhale without smelling anything and to convince herself that she was not swallowing other people's air-borne filth. She was so relieved when the officer at the desk called her name that she got up very quickly, nudged the large lady and knocked off the young man's cap. The large lady uttered some small obscenity under her breath while the young man shouted across the room,

"Ignorant fuckin' bitch! Watch where you're fuckin' goin' or I'll bang ya next time!"

The officer at the desk shouted a warning to the young man and got a raised middle finger as a reply. Helen did not know where to put herself having never been in a police station before. She spoke very quietly at the desk and the officer had to lean forward and tilt his head slightly to hear her. Eventually, she was buzzed through a metal detecting doorframe to a side room.

A policewoman asked her for her name, address and date of birth. Helen answered nervously and stood shivering as she waited, not knowing what to expect. The computer beeped as the policewoman read something from the screen and nodded.

"Don't be nervous ma'am," reassured the policewoman, "just go through to the interview room and take a seat on this side of the table. Someone will be along to speak with you shortly," the officer said as she pointed out the door behind her.

Helen held onto her bag with both hands in front of her and walked quite slowly. When she pushed open the door she saw a small, well-lit room with nothing in it save a table, four chairs and a recording device built into the wall. There was a large mirror on the far wall, which she assumed to be one-way glass, reflecting her nervous posture. Next to the mirror was a solid door. The door shut behind her with a definite click and the door opposite opened almost simultaneously as a man in a suit walked in.

"Hello Miss Waters, I'm Detective Inspector Thompson, how may I help today?" he stated as he removed his jacket and sat at the table, offering a seat to Helen with his open hand.

Helen could not help but look at the detective for a moment with an unmoving facial expression that was disrespectfully close to being a rude stare. She tried hard to nationalise his skin tone and features but being somewhat ignorant of the complexities of ethnicity she could not place him. His accent was definitely local, although anyone from another ethnic group was difficult to find in this predominantly white British society and Helen was unaccustomed to such encounters. She introduced herself to the detective and nervously explained all about Tom and the confessions he had made to her. She presented him with the printouts she had from the media files and some of the notes she had made from Tom's file. Thompson thumbed through the pages, nodding his head and fanning out some of the sheets. Helen sat in silence and looked at the files upside down as the detective read them through.

"This is very thorough, Miss Waters, you have obviously been looking into this."

When he had read the documents, or at least scanned enough of them to gain an insight into their content, he leaned forward towards Helen.

"I can't do anything about this right now due to a lack of my knowledge about this case, but what I can do is pass this on to our Cold Case Team and they will talk to you at their earliest convenience."

He looked her in the eye and appeared sincere.

"If you are genuinely concerned then we are genuinely concerned. We will do all we can to help you, Miss Waters."

The detective double-checked the contact numbers for Helen and wrote down her work address. Only slightly reassured by his sincerity, she thanked the detective as they stood up at the same time and shook hands.

* * * * *

Jodie was still holding the phone even though the caller had hung up. She stood motionless, entranced by the buzzing dialling tone as she stared at the wall. Connor was running through the hall pushing a small pushchair with a soft toy in it and accidentally banged into the doorframe every time he went hurtling past. The sound of the hard plastic wheels as they clacked over the wooden floor echoed with the shrieks of excitement soon became a cacophony that Jodie could no longer bare. Suddenly, she screamed like she had never screamed before,

"STOP IT!" she trailed off into tears, and slammed the phone in place.

Connor stopped in his tracks, like a rabbit caught in the headlights of impending doom. He stared at his mummy in disbelief as his lower lip quivered before he burst into tears himself. Jodie fell to her knees and embraced her son and the two inconsolable souls cried in unison.

The doorbell was only noticed after the third attempt and it had been joined by a loud knock. Jodie wiped her face on her sleeves and stepped over Connor to get to the door. She opened it slightly and looked out through a narrow gap. When she saw the police uniforms she opened the door wide and invited them in. Jodie knew why they were here and explained that Natalie had called to tell her the news.

"We have reason to believe," started the police woman, "that Elsie has been taken against her will, although we have no idea why. Does she have any enemies?"

Jodie smiled and shook her head, "How can she have enemies? She's a frail old lady who harms nobody. How is she going to find time to make enemies?"

She cried again. Connor heard his mother's sadness and instinctively came into the room and curled up next to her like a lost puppy. He too sobbed in sympathy for his mummy. Jodie wrapped an arm around his shoulders and stroked him reassuringly with her thumb. The second constable leaned forward and asked some questions about the last time she saw Elsie and what the conversation was about. Jodie explained everything and everything seemed normal.

"May we talk to your partner? Mr Graham Rice, is it?"

"Yes, that's right, but I'm afraid he's not here right now. He plays golf on Sunday's and he turns his mobile off so he can get away from work," she explained.

"When may we reach him?" the constable pushed, leaning further forward.

"He will be home around four, usually. Depends how well he does and how many they have at the nineteenth," Jodie shrugged.

"Which course is he on? The Greenfield's Memorial or Dale View?"

"Dale View. He's a member there," Jodie shrugged and began to sob again.

Jodie talked with the female constable as the young man radioed in the details. They left a card with contact numbers with Jodie and asked her to call if she remembered anything important or had any further information. When the officers had gone, Jodie was trapped in the emptiness around her. Her home felt alien to her now without any form of comfort. She stepped over toys where once she would have gathered them up and packed them away. Distant and unsure, she walked up and down her stairs and in and out of rooms with neither direction nor purpose. She found herself standing still for a moment or two before walking on to somewhere else, equally aimless and void of thought. Weeping constantly, she eventually came to rest halfway up the stairs where she sat with her back to the wall, hugging her legs with her head on her knees. Connor had taken out more toys from his toybox and was playing with a car as if nothing had happened. He pushed it back and forth over the tiled floor in the kitchen making loud 'vroom vroom' noises. Jodie sat on the stairs, listening and weeping.

* * * * *

Helen was sat in her favourite position in her favourite chair watching her favourite soap. She was so comfortable here she was blissfully unaware of her surroundings and had temporarily discarded her haunting thoughts. Totally engrossed, she stared intently at the screen. There had been an argument in a pub and the landlord had told his daughter that she was not his and that she had been adopted as a baby. His wife had overheard the conversation and screamed at the father as the daughter stormed out the door. Although Helen's mind was pre-occupied with nagging thoughts of reality, it was all very exciting for her. She took the lives of these characters very seriously. It was a long scene and became very heated. The acting was quite intense, for a soap opera, Helen thought. Nathan stared at the television; not really knowing who was who and what and why, but carefully watching the people move around a lot and shout at each other. The scene before him seemed to be digging into his psyche, much to his surprise, and he was actually moved by what was going on. His thoughts were most definitely provoked and on a journey elsewhere; somewhere he wasn't sure he wanted to go. He shuffled in his seat once or twice, and then took a deep intake of breath.

"I was adopted."

His voice wavered as if buckling under the weight of the emotion it carried. He felt sad, embarrassed and yet strangely relieved on hearing those words out loud. They hung in the air in front of him, out in the open, beckoning Helen for a response. Helen was taken aback. Where had that come from? He very rarely, if ever, spoke of his childhood or his family and now he drops the biggest bombshell since they met. Although something in his disclosure made her feel warm and needed by her lover, too many clouds obscured her sunshine and she wasn't sure how to cope with this conversation right now. There was enough going on in her mind without this overflowing her. She snapped away from the story on the television, turned to Nathan and questioned,

"What?"

A brief silence.

"I was adopted."

He turned to face her as he began to feel more comfortable, although he was still a little unsure of himself. He dropped his eyes from her gaze.

"My mother gave me up and left me to someone else."

Helen dropped her chin and raised her eyebrows. She didn't know what to say. She reached over for the remote control and turned off the television. Stunned, she sat in silence while she listened to Nathan tell her the story of his childhood. He told of how he had been passed from one foster home to another until he finally got adopted. How he changed schools every term and never made any real long-term friends until secondary school. Several years ago, when Nathan was a teenager, he had traced his mother. He had found out where she was living but had never plucked up the courage to go and meet her. Nathan told Helen all about his teenage years, his home in the village and his friends at Camthorpe Technology School. He explained that his adopted parents were very good to him and he loved them dearly. He treated them as if they were his natural parents and they treated him as if he were their natural child. His family life was settled, secure and loving. It was not long after he left home for university that they divorced. The whole affair was unexpected and emotionally tumultuous for both Nathan and his adopted mother. She fell ill soon after and never really recovered. She had told him that his father had left her for another woman, but the rumours in the village were that it was actually for another man. Nathan left university shortly after his first year to stay home and look after his mother during her illness. She died two long and lonely years later after never really making any kind of recovery. His father never showed up at the funeral but it was well attended. His mother was very popular in the village; she had a small flower shop and shared coffee mornings with the other women of her age. The funeral took place on a quiet day, without any sign of describable weather, at the local church. Nathan remembered that there was nothing distinctive about anything that day; it was bland and non-descript, which, ironically, is what made it so memorable.

"She would have liked it that way. No fuss," said Nathan quietly, almost crying.

Nathan had inherited the house and a reasonable sum of money in the will. The shop was given to a niece, Nathan's only cousin. His father was at the solicitor's office when the will was read, but they didn't speak to each other. His father got nothing from her at all, which angered him and pleased Nathan. Nathan intended to go back to university but his new-found wealth and recent loss had made him somewhat reclusive in the first instance and he talked himself out of the idea. He began to drink heavily and became very generous, especially after a few pints of hand-pulled cask ale, and often bought rounds for the pub regulars. It was through his generosity with alcohol that he made some unsavoury friends.

One night, after a heavy drinking session, he was staggering home with two of his friends from the city. They were singing loudly in the street and laughing. Passers by crossed the road to get out of the way of the verbal abuse they were being subjected to. When the three of them staggered upon the sidings of a busy main road, they leaned themselves up against the railings, still singing loudly and joking offensively. They swayed there for a while with clumsy feet falling off the floor as they desperately stamped out for firmer ground. They loudly debated how to get to the other side of this four-lane super-highway to reach the sanctuary of the well-lit bus stop. Gary relieved himself into the gutter as he shouted loudly and invited all passers by to admire his marvellous manhood.

The road was quite busy, even at such a late hour. It started to rain, lightly at first, but it soon got heavy. Within minutes the three friends were soaked through to the skin and squinting from the rain. Nathan put his arm around the shoulders of his friend Mark and together they meandered their way towards a subway just a few stumbled paces down the street. Gary had decided, in all his drunken stupidity, to take a short cut. He had pulled himself up and over the railing, slipped into his own piss-puddle and rolled into the road, still laughing. When he stood up, he turned around to face his two friends. He swung round too fast and realised that the beer had stolen his balance. He fell headlong onto the railing and banged his head. He slumped backwards and lay across the inside lane of the road. Nathan and Mark were laughing hysterically as they started back towards Gary. When they noticed Gary was hurt and no longer laughing, they began to sober up quickly and walked a little faster and straighter. He was rubbing his head and had started to get up slowly. Just as they came alongside the railings next to Gary, the night was split by the sound of screeching brakes and the smell of burning rubber. There was a horrible wet thud as a van hit Gary. The impact lifted him off the road, right in front of Nathan and Mark, and scooped him across the inside lane. His body was thrown across the railings, lifeless and limp, bloodied and torn. His broken torso rolled and bounced along the hard, wet ground before splashing down in the flooded gutter as Nathan and Mark stared helplessly. The crippled carcass was bent out of shape and didn't seem human anymore. His arms and legs were folded at unnatural angles and there were chunks of flesh and blood splashed in its wake. Mark was instantly sick on the grass verge, with Nathan following after. The world had started to spin violently. The driver of the van was screaming at the two young men although they could not make any sense of what he was saying. The sound of the cars had become a dull roar as the world around them slowed down. All sounds became booming and long. Time stopped and the air became unbearably heavy. It seemed like they had become trapped in a timeless nightmare with no escape. Even the harsh rain was irrelevant now despite every drop stinging into their faces and beating down their brows.

The emergency rescue vehicles had appeared out of nowhere to break the evil spell and the whole night had been lit up with flashing blue lights. The sound of the rain had become crackled with the faint sound of police radios. Just as slowly as it had stopped, the world around them speeded up again as it tried desperately to resume normal service at its regular pace.

Nathan said he could remember every last detail of that night and he would never forget it. He had dreamed the whole sequence every night for several months after and had needed continuous counselling. After a long silence and still not making eye contact with Helen, he got up and left the room. He wiped his face as he was leaving, trying not to show his obvious sadness.

"Do you want a cup of tea?" he asked, his voice shaking as he tried to smile it out.

"I'll do it love. You come and sit down," Helen got up and walked after him.

She saw him in the kitchen, acting as if nothing had been said, singing a silly song about the kettle and the milk. Helen questioned him, but Nathan just stared and shook his head. He went back to his song. She really wanted to hold him, be there for him, love him, but he was not open to it. He didn't want to show himself at all. One minute he had opened his personal firewall and now all of a sudden he had bolted the gates. He dismissed all Helen's efforts to engage in conversation about his youth to the point of being rude, abrupt and upsetting to Helen.

When they returned to the room, it was Nathan that put the television back on and channel hopped until he found something he thought he might like. Helen looked up at the time and checked her watch against the clock. She wound it a bit, just in case, and sat down for her tea. Her head was swimming but Nathan didn't seem bothered at all. It was as if he had just switched it off completely. It was his skill of hiding his emotions that Helen was quite jealous of if she was honest to herself, even though she hated when he did it. It seemed that many people around Helen had the ability to control their emotions and they affected them, to the point where she thought there must be something wrong with her. Sometimes she wished she could just turn off the negativity in her life, but she kept hold of things too closely and became 'emotionally involved', which according to Nathan was a sign of weakness.

They sat in silence for almost an hour, watching a documentary based on the videos taken by police patrol cars on duty. Both Helen and Nathan were feeling uncomfortable watching, but neither one dared to speak to the other for fear of starting up an emotionally charged conversation that neither one of them were prepared to enter into. Instead, they avoided the subject, shuffling in their seats, sighing occasionally and running their fingers through their hair. The atmosphere was charged and delicate. Helen was the first one to surrender and feel the need to break the silence.

"Do you think it's strange that if you have something going on in your life, it seems to get reflected on the TV?" Helen questioned, "I mean, you got something on your mind and there it is in the soap or on the news or something. Do you think it's a bit … spooky?"

Nathan looked at Helen through squinted eyes, his head tilted. He leaned over to her, put one arm around her shoulder and gave a gentle kiss on the cheek.

"Helen, you're my girl and I love you very much, but you are too damn superstitious!" he said sarcastically, "There's nothing spooky or … or … you know … in this life."

He knew what he was trying to say and so did Helen,

"Just that the TV show stirred up a few memories and I got caught up in the moment, nothing to worry about. It's over now," he added, "and we need never mention it again."

He sat back on the settee and began to flick through the channels again. Helen just looked at him. He had completely blocked out the event, as easily as blowing out a candle. She could still feel it, still hear his words and see the poor man's body in the road, but Nathan had turned it all off. He seemed to be completely detached from it now.

"It's just that Tom at work explained that he had a child, unknown to him and it got adopted out. I just got wondering, that's all."

She shrugged her shoulders, made herself comfortable on the settee and turned to face Nathan. He knew this meant he was going to be talked to so he lowered the volume on the television and turned to face Helen, braced himself and looked as attentive as he possibly could. Helen explained all about Tom and the events around him meeting the mother of his child after such a long time. She left out the bit where he tampered with the needle, because she could not cope with his reaction right now, but she did tell him all about the drugs and the lifestyle changes before and after the baby.

Helen went on to talk about Elsie and how she came to be looking after Jodie, but she could see that Nathan had begun to lose interest and his attention was slowly but surely being dragged back to the television. She dropped in a random comment about a monkey in the CD player, just to check if he was paying attention. Sure enough, Nathan just nodded in agreement. As she suspected, he was not listening and made no attempt to find out what she had said. Helen shook her head, sighed and turned to face the television.

The Crawler was on the news again. He had been seen several times running through gardens in an affluent part of town and hanging around the Halls of Residence of the local university. The police still had no further information about him and the reporters kept on regurgitating the same old information, each time trying to make it sound like there had been a breakthrough of some sort. They reported that he was athletic as he had jumped over fences, climbed walls and run long distances to evade recognition. Nathan tutted at the story and shook his head a lot, his anger rose at the newsreader,

"How many times are you going to tell us he wears black clothes and a black ski mask? That he's the average size of every other male?" he said to the television before he turned to Helen, "They won't catch him, you know. Even if they do, it'll be a short sentence and he'll serve less than half of it. They don't enforce laws these days - too expensive. A bloke can get away with murder if he wanted to."

"Yeah" was her only response.

Helen just nodded and started picking at her fingernails, trying desperately to get Nathan to notice that she wanted to be listened to. She wanted him to ask her "what's up?" but he didn't realise. He did not have a clue that she needed him and she added his oblivious nonchalance to her list of doubts, that slowly but surely were damaging her feelings towards him. Nathan slumped back into the settee again and flicked from one channel to the next as he moaned that there was nothing on any of the hundred or so channels. The conversation never really picked up again. Helen toyed with her fingers for a while and then turned her attention to her feet. After a quick moment, she wandered off to the bathroom for some more serious pampering with her pedicure set. Nathan heard the familiar sound of the bath running and waited for the door to shut with the usual clicks and the slide of the bolt. He lowered the volume on the television so that he could only just hear what was being said and then quickly flicked over to the soft porn channel that came on after the sports channel had signed off for the night. He settled back to watch some scantily clad lesbians acting out sex with each other in soft focus. The music was terrible, the acting was awful and the sex wasn't real, but Nathan got aroused anyway. It was not long before he heard Helen leaving the bathroom and making her way across to the bedroom. Nathan paced up and down the living room, desperately wanting relief but knowing that Helen would not be receptive to his approaches.

* * * * *

Lucy left the Home cheerfully, thankful that her long day was over, and headed out through the gardens towards the main road at the front of the building. There was a full moon and the sky was full of stars. Lucy watched as her shadows grew and circled around her as she walked through the soft pools of light cast by the Victorian styled lampposts along the path, then they disappeared underneath her to go around again as she walked. She fumbled through the pocket of her coat and pulled out her mp3 player. She unravelled the headphones and secured them in her ears. The subtle sounds of the night were instantly replaced with the soulful ambience of Something Pretty. They were one of Lucy's favourite bands; they sang harmoniously about the joys and woes of eternal love to the sound of softly strummed acoustic guitars. Lucy smiled a little and began to whisper the words; her soft breath appeared wisp-like with every line. She buried her hands deep into her warm pockets, snuggling them down into the soft corners of the thick, woollen material. As she pushed down with her hands, her collar rubbed up against the back of her neck and made her shake her head slowly with a secure smile. As she came out of the gardens and onto the main road, she paused to look left and right. The streets were unusually quiet. Lucy often walked home at the same time each night and could keep track of the time depending on where the regular passers-by were in their own routines. The red car that usually passed her at the end of the road was nowhere in sight although for several nights previous it had just arrived at the junction, almost as if it had been waiting for her before it went on its way. The dog-walker appeared right on cue at the far end of the road with the bouncing golden retriever sniffing and running alongside, fading away into the distance. She turned to walk on and watched her shadows again. She felt the cold of the early autumn air embrace her so she pulled the belt on her coat tighter around her middle and folded up her collar against her neck, bringing back another smile of comfort.

Suddenly she noticed another shadow growing next to hers but before she could do or say anything, a gloved hand clamped over her mouth and pulled out one of her earpieces as another arm clung around her waist. Swiftly, she was swept up off the floor and carried along through the air. She tried to scream but the sounds were muffled in the leather of the glove. In a desperate attempt to break away from his grip, she shook her head frantically to no avail. She threw her arms and legs back and forth, as if running, with no effect. She was dragged through a hedgerow and into a wheat field.

"Don't scream. There's no one around!" growled a voice in her ear.

Lucy could feel the warm woollen mask rub against her ear, cheek and neck as he spoke and a cold wave of fear shot through her like a flash of lightening from her heart to her extremities. The pair stumbled, as if dancing a chilling misplaced waltz on uneven ground, and then suddenly, like pins at the mercy of a well-aimed strike, they fell to the floor. Lucy struggled all the while, with diminishing effort as she drained herself of strength. Now and again she shook free of the glove and her screams escaped unheard into the night. The lead from the headphones had wrapped around her neck and she felt it tight against her; the wire hot and sharp against her skin. She was forced face down on the hard mud as the buckled remains of the harvested wheat scratched into her face and legs. He was on top of her with her mouth still clamped in the leather glove. His other hand pulled at her coat and popped the buttons. He fumbled around his own waist to remove his belt then he clawed at her apron. Layers of clothes rubbed against each other, gathered in creases and then gave way at the seams. She felt him under her skirt as he pulled at her knickers. The lace tore and she felt the elastic rub down her thigh, the heat of the friction was startling against the cool night air on her exposed buttocks. Her mind was alight with fear. She struggled even more as she felt his hand feeling between her legs, invading.

"Good girl, good girl!" growled the voice again.

She forced her head round to one side and lost the grip of the glove, which had become moist from her sweat and saliva. She caught a few successive deep breaths and focussed her efforts for a short time but before she could make any attempt at retaliation or defence, she felt him grab her hair behind her head. He pulled sharply upwards as he gripped her tightly and a sharp, hot sensation flashed across her scalp seconds before he smashed her forehead down into the dry stubble. She gasped and lay still for a moment and then her nose suddenly became warm and blocked. She could feel him struggling behind her, his hands between her legs, assaulting her and stabbing unimaginable discomfort into her anus. Her eyes welled with tears, her face stinging with scratches. The sounds of the night had been drowned with the sounds of her terror, clawing and fighting, shrouding and smothering. Struggling for breath, she gargled through her blood as it ran back down her throat from her nose. Her thoughts raced and her fear rose in her like a fire burning loudly and building up pressure.

"Oh my god, oh my god, oh my god!" her thoughts screamed as she felt his fingers inside her.

The living nightmare ripped through her head, piercing her ears, fanning the flames of her horror. Lucy's thoughts flew to her family, her mother and father, her little sister. Her fear grew, transmogrified and emerged like a phoenix with a wake of pure anger.

She felt herself growing in size as she gained strength. Spitting blood and gathering her breath, she threw herself about; her arms, her legs, her head; in any direction at all as if caught in a violent seizure. She managed to throw him off and spin over onto her back but he grabbed out for her again and caught hold of her leg. For an instant, their eyes met. His piercing stare burned through the eye slit of his black ski mask. She sat up and lashed out with her arms knocking him backward with her increasing strength.

"Bitch!" he spat through his woollen mask.

She jumped up quick while he was laid on his back on the hard, sharp ground. Through her tear stained eyes, her dizziness and confusion, she could see the soft outline of his exposed erect penis in the light of the full moon. She stamped down hard, her anger gathered into her heel and released at the point of impact. The softness of the fleshy organ at the mercy of her furious foot gave way as she met the solidity of the pelvic bone. He bent double almost instantly; his knees came up toward his chest like a bear trap trying to catch the offending limb. A long gargled scream faded into the fields until he fell silent and out of breath. He collapsed in a heap with both hands covering his genitals.

Lucy had gathered all of her strength now and began to run back towards the hedgerow, stumbling here and there as her uncertain feet battled with the uneven field. She forced her way through the wall of foliage, already damaged and snapped by their entrance, without a care for the scratches she could feel cutting into her face, hands and legs. She fell out of the bush in a heap on the tarmac path as she broke out from the world of horror behind the hedge. Dizzy and disorientated, she got to her feet slowly and realised that she had lost a shoe and her foot was bleeding quite badly. The lead from the headphones was still wrapped around her neck and hurt her now although she could not feel it a moment ago. She ripped it away in an instant. It burned her flesh as the wire stretched under the tension before snapping away. She looked through the hedge to the field beyond and saw his dark silhouette still rocking back and forth on the floor. The elastic of her knickers was wrapped around one ankle; the material had been torn along the seams. She shook her foot a couple of times and the tattered remains came away forming a delicate pile of lace on the course black path. She straightened her clothes as best she could before staggering off quickly in the direction of the Home she had just left. The journey was a blur of lights, shadows and painful limbs. Nightmare images and phantom sensations haunted her imagination. Pains rose to the surface and then dived again to attack her internally. Aching bruises grew unseen on her flesh. Blood stung as it seeped its way into the scratches to begin the healing of the wounds as she faded to black.

When Lucy woke she was in a room at the home, laid on a bed. Two of her colleagues and a man she didn't recognise were standing over her. She sat up quickly and screamed.

"It's OK, Lucy, you're safe now," assured Marie as she gathered her up in a hug and let her cry into her chest.

Lucy sobbed loudly while the people in the room tried to console her. The man she didn't recognise introduced himself as Detective Inspector Thompson and his colleague was WPC Jordan. Lucy lay back on the bed and continued her inconsolable crying.

"We need to know…" started WPC Jordan.

"A man attacked me in the street outside and dragged me into the field. I've lost my mp3!" cried Lucy.

Lucy collapsed again and Marie hugged her. She had to hold her tight to keep her shivering from overwhelming the two women. The detective and his companion explained that they needed to find out what had happened as soon as possible so they could try to get any forensic evidence they could.

"We can take DNA evidence anything up to a week after the event, but the sooner the better for more accurate match," Thompson explained to Marie.

After almost an hour of crying and consolation Lucy began to explain the incident in a random order, with different memories springing up at different times. Her voice was shaking and she kept breaking into tears, which left Marie's blouse wet and smeared with make up. Marie's own fear rose inside her as she thought of the Crawler being in the vicinity of the Home. For Lucy's sake, she tried to focus on the moment and shudder away the horrors of what may be outside in the darkness. It took until dawn to get the story in order. The detective asked WPC Jordan to radio in for a search party to scour the area in the field. Everybody was asked to leave the room and a police examiner spoke with Lucy in private while taking evidence from her body.

"I want Marie here," whimpered Lucy through her tears.

It was a harrowing experience being a crime scene and having her wounds photographed. She flinched whenever the WPC touched her. Every now and again, a scene from the nightmare she had just survived flashed in front of her eyes in every detail and caused her to jolt away from the WPC. It was a long slow process interrupted with tears and whimpering screams. Marie held her hand throughout and cried silently to herself as she tried so hard to stay strong for Lucy. WPC Jordan gently held Lucy's hand and checked her nails for evidence. There were traces of blood in with the soil. The WPC smiled to Lucy as she took the swab.

"We will get him," she nodded reassuringly.

The assurance meant nothing to Lucy. There was no justice on Earth that could allow her to feel vindicated after what he had done to her. Eventually, after the high drama and lengthy questioning, everybody left and Marie sat with Lucy. She slept while Marie bathed her wounds, crying softly.

Helen was pottering in the kitchen while eating a warm round of toast when she heard a knock at the front door. She wiped her buttery hands on a tea towel as she hurried through the hall with a sense of urgency. She opened the door with an automatic "hello."

"Hello, Miss Waters? I am Inspector Davis and this is PC Reid, from the Cold Case Review Team. I believe you are expecting us?" the first man stated, raising an open wallet with a photograph and badge, "may we come in?"

Helen showed the two men through to the living room and made them each a cup of tea as they informed Helen that they had been advised to make enquiries after her visit to the station. The three sat and sipped their drinks intermittently as they spoke. The inspector placed a cardboard wallet full of dog-eared paperwork on the table. It was held shut by two elastic straps, stretched to their limits, over the bottom corners.

"Now we have seen your file and we are very impressed with your findings," nodded the Inspector in unison with his colleague.

"As you know, we have an active Crawler at present, he's been in the news a lot," he added as he placed his tea on a coaster and leaned forward towards Helen.

"We are not releasing this to the press but we suspect we have something of a copy-cat on our hands," he said in a quieter voice.

He sat back and spoke slightly louder, "Now you know the history of the case. Adam Wright was arrested…."

"Adam Wright?" interrupted Helen, "I thought nobody had been charged. The Garden Creeper just disappeared?"

"Yes, yes…" he nodded knowingly and rubbed his chin, "that's as far as the original investigation went but then he killed two young people in a horrific act and was arrested shortly after. His name was Adam Wright, coincidentally enough he was the man that discovered the body of Amanda Wilkinson; the overdose case also in your file."

"My God!" Helen raised a hand over her mouth as specks of the awful truth fell into place.

"He protested his innocence," started PC Reid, "but his DNA was all over the murder scene and quite a few of the Garden Creeper crime scenes too. When we told him we had a pretty good match on the DNA he changed his story and blamed his father."

Helen felt feint. The room began to sway like a boat lost at sea.

"Yes," agreed the Inspector, "he developed a long and complicated story about him being adopted and his natural mother, Amanda, was killed by his natural father, who he never actually met. Convenient eh? We looked into the death of Ms Wilkinson but we found no reason to suspect foul play. In the absence of any tangible evidence and no post mortem, we left the case as is without reopening it."

Helen was intrigued as to why he could have protested his innocence against DNA evidence; she was a firm believer that if DNA was present then the case was all but solved.

"DNA evidence is such a fragile thing you see. In the good old days, when this science was new, it was generally believed that DNA was solid proof but unfortunately we have become victims of our own success. We can analyse things in much greater detail which, ironically, gives us a wider margin of error," the officer gesticulated a lot as he spoke, waving his hands around to emphasise detail.

"For example," he began as he shuffled in his seat, "imagine we get a 95-100% hit every time we use this evidence. That sets a pretty high standard does it not?"

Helen nodded.

"So then, when we get a 70-80% hit then questions are asked. It's these slight variations that bring in a shadow of doubt and that is why, in several cases that do not have a 100% match, the DNA evidence is either questioned and dismissed, or just not put forward to the courts. In this case, the DNA evidence was 'polluted' if you like, and difficult to isolate exactly."

"And there are plenty of egotistical solicitors that just love to exercise their legal expertise to get people off, even when they are guilty!" added Reid.

"Quite. We believed Adam's solicitors were aware of this and used it to his advantage to emphasise to the jury that there was some area of doubt," he added.

The inspector shuffled forward in his seat. They talked about the psychological profile and the childhood of Adam as they continued their drinks. It was evident that Adam was a mixed up young man with a deep-rooted hatred of women, probably because of his broken relationship with his mother and a whole web of issues around attachment and loss, in conjunction with his adoption. It all sounded like psychobabble to Helen, but it was an all too familiar story based on several high-profile cases.

"Yes, apparently he had seen a man at the house of his alleged mother and suspected he was his natural father," the inspector pulled out a couple of sheets of paper from the file, "ah yes, here it is. It says in Adam's statement that he suspected him of being the father but never found out his name. He overheard some of the argument they were having inside when he was at the door before he ran away. He followed the man around … on and off for months after … found out where he lived … kept tabs on him, so he claimed," offered the inspector, "he even kept a diary of this other man's comings and goings, though his identity was never confirmed."

"Adam insisted that he wanted to confront him, to speak with him, but he claims that he never plucked up the courage," added PC Reid.

"So the Garden Creeper could have been someone else then? It could have been his father?" asked Helen.

"Well, theoretically speaking yes, but I must say that is highly unlikely. Adam Wright was a very mixed up individual and eventually committed suicide while in prison. He swore he was innocent until his final day; in fact his suicide note just said 'It wasn't me'," shrugged the officer as he raised the file and patted it lightly with his palm.

"Now you have come along and brought us this information about this old man Tom, we will have to investigate. This case has been officially reopened."

* * * * *

The St Anthony of Padua Home for the Elderly was unusually busy throughout the morning. Police Officers talked to staff and took notes. The CCTV footage for the previous week was being scrutinised by a young officer in plain clothes. He watched the monitor intently in a room behind reception while he made detailed notes of his observations. One of the offices off the main reception had been sign-posted as a restricted area and the single police officer standing guard outside ensured no unauthorised personnel entered the designated Incident Room. People walked here and there with an increased sense of urgency. They talked on corners and whispered in corridors. The atmosphere was tense and forced all those entering it into an apprehensive silence. The seating areas in the wide reception hall had been selected for questioning staff and visitors and some had temporary dividers erected around them for privacy.

Police officers sat at various points conversing with visitors and residents alike. They jotted down notes and muttered into radios. All members of the public visiting their relatives were taken aside to have their contact details written down after their brief questioning. Worried residents frowned at each other and shook their heads as they went out through reception and into the gardens talking and speculating wildly. The facts of the case were unknown to most people in the building but the rumours had already taken hold, swayed judgements and created incredible fantasies.

DI Thompson had called in Jodie and her partner Graham for questioning. They were in the main reception area, sat on a red leather couch with dark wood detailing while the detective sat opposite on a matching coffee table. He had a writing pad in one hand and a chewed disposable pen in the other. He discussed various details with Jodie and Graham, although Jodie was doing most of the answering while Graham just sat there listening nervously. He shuffled in his seat and was obviously in some discomfort. The questioning became emotional now and again and Jodie had to pause for a sip of water and to wipe her tears with her tissue.

"We have reason to believe that you are the only living relative, Miss Manning, is that true?"

"Yes," replied Jodie, "why?"

"Because, and please forgive me, we have also ascertained that Elsie had quite a fortune and…"

"How dare you!" screamed Jodie, causing all within earshot to turn their gaze in her direction, "I would never have done anything..."

Graham took hold of Jodie and she fell silent as the attention of the surrounding eyes fell back onto their own business. He put his arms around her and hugged her to him, scowling at the detective and shaking his head. His stare was uncharacteristically sinister for such an awkward looking man and Thompson was taken aback by it.

"I'm so sorry, Miss Manning, but we have to rule out all possibilities. I know this is a difficult time but there will be uncomfortable questions being asked. We have to check everything out, however unthinkable it may be for you," his tone was level and well practised.

DI Thompson harboured feelings of sorrow for Jodie. He somehow knew she was a suspect by default only and was not capable of doing anything remotely criminal, especially towards her dearest Aunt Elsie. He realised his attraction to her was bordering on unprofessional in time to stop himself falling any deeper into her red-rimmed tear-stained eyes. He was drawn to her, she was beautiful to him and his protective masculine instincts had gone into overdrive since he had met her. His gaze lingered on her for a few moments before he turned his attention to Graham and altered his mood to suit the line of questioning. Graham squirmed in his seat and grimaced slightly as he stared back at Thompson.

"We tried to contact you at the golf course on Sunday morning but you were not there, sir. Can you tell me where you were?"

"I was … out … all morning," he stuttered, "on the golf course."

"Sir, we contacted the staff there and they confirmed that even though you are a member you hardly ever visit the course. They informed us that you only ever play golf on your own on the very rare occasions that you do play."

Graham gritted his teeth, shook his head and glared at the detective. Jodie looked on, slightly aghast.

"I was …" he stuttered and paused, "… out walking on the course. I sometimes just walk out there to clear my head," he added, nodding, his voice trailed off into a whisper as his gaze dropped to the floor.

"Can anyone confirm that?" asked the detective as he wrote it in his book, shaking his head.

"A couple of golfers saw me, I don't know who they were."

Jodie began to cry even harder and thumped Graham's arm feebly as he held on to her. Her thoughts raced as they ploughed over her emotions. Something was wrong, Jodie could feel it, something somewhere was amiss but she couldn't put her finger on it. She hated him right now for not sharing everything with her. When she attempted to speak her emotion choked her as her tears came flooding down her face and she collapsed into a heap against Graham. His arms embraced her and he rested his chin on her head as she cried into his chest.

Helen appeared as a black outline against the autumnal sun streaming in through the large doorway. She was bewildered by the vivacious upheaval of the room and after her initial light-headedness in the kafuffle, honed-in on DI Thompson. She walked over to the group while she looked around at the various activities taking place just about everywhere. The detective rose to his feet and greeted her. Jodie remained slouched and Graham held on to her. Helen noticed Graham and recognised him as the man she had seen in the restaurant with Lucy. Her mouth opened slightly as she realised that he had recently asked Jodie to marry him yet he was taking another woman out on a date. Helen had met Jodie many times and couldn't help but notice how distraught she was, which she thought odd. Graham glared at Helen, his forehead furrowed and his eyebrows tensed over his squinted eyes. She felt very uncomfortable in the glare and turned to the detective, confused. The detective explained to Helen about Elsie disappearing and the attack on Lucy. Helen listened in disbelief and as the realisation of what had occurred sunk in she became nauseous. Her legs became weak and she felt an irresistible urge to sit down. The only space was on the other side of Graham and with him glaring at her with what she perceived to be malicious intent she decided against it and walked to a matching couch on the other side of the table. Helen's head swam in a whirlpool of information and she felt her weight disappear from her as she fell into the couch.

Jodie began to cry harder, her upper body shuddered as she listened to the details regarding her Aunt's disappearance. Graham was trying to console her. His face had returned to its usual passive, clumsy self. All the while, Helen looked from one to the other and back again.

"Lucy?" quivered Helen.

"She's in the Health Unit," he pointed down the corridor, "she was too afraid to leave the building last night and nobody thought it would have been in her best interests to have gone home with a colleague, so she stayed here. She's traumatised but stable. Her physical state is not too bad; some cuts and bruises, a broken nose but nothing life threatening. She will recover from that but I'm afraid it's the emotional damage that will take time to heal," he spoke calmly and sincerely.

"Can we talk about the other matter, please?" asked Helen, motioning the detective to leave the seating area and find somewhere more private.

Thompson noticed she was looking over at Graham with worried eyes and so he stood up. Helen rose too and the detective took hold of her elbow for emotional support. They walked slowly a few paces away from the table and made their way towards a cold water dispenser against the wall.

"I saw Graham out with Lucy on Friday night. No, sorry, it was Saturday, Saturday night. She was out with him on a date, she told me when we talked in the Ladies," Helen spoke quickly and quietly, hoping not to be overheard.

Thompson slipped a plastic cup out of the cylinder and began to siphon a drink from the tap. He turned to Helen as he took a sip. He saw over Helen's shoulder that Jodie had stood up and walked toward the water cooler, staring at Helen. Helen turned to look, swallowed hard and anticipated an emotional exchange of words.

"Did I hear you right?" asked Jodie, angrily, "My Graham was out with another woman?"

Graham covered his face with his hands and rocked back and forth on the couch, growling into his palms.

"I'm so sorry, I … didn't want ... I tried …" stuttered Helen.

"Are you saying Graham was out on a date with someone else?" she asked getting angrier, turning her attention to Graham, who was growing red in the face.

"I'm so sorry!" Helen started, "He was out with Lucy in Bellino's on Saturday night. I saw him clearly and spoke to Lucy too. My partner Nathan can confirm it," she added, nodding to the detective. She spoke quickly as if to get it over with as soon as possible.

No sooner had Helen mentioned Nathan's name than she remembered the way he had recognised Lucy too. How did he know her? Her thoughts raced but the immediate situation played on her fears. She shut down the stream of thought and returned her focus to Jodie.

"You asked me to marry you!" she screamed at Graham.

She struggled to tug the ring from her finger and threw it towards Graham. He dodged to the left as it bounced off the settee and out into the middle of the floor. Jodie backed away and her face slowly transformed from anger to sadness as she began to cry and fell back into the couch. She raised her hands over her mouth and stared at Helen in disbelief as floods of tears covered her red face. Graham stood up angrily and he threw his fists in the air, staring at Helen.

"You fucking bitch!" he shouted, spitting as he spoke.

All eyes in the room turned to Graham and two uniformed officers, responding to the developing hostility, started quickly towards the group. Graham's face had shaded to purple and his veins in his forehead bulged under the pressure. He quickly pulled off his glasses and spat more obscenities at Helen. DI Thompson stepped in between Helen and Graham and raised his hands.

"Calm down sir, if you continue like this, I will have you arrested!" he insisted.

Graham tried shouting over the shoulder of the tall detective but his advances were blocked. After a few more obscenities and outbursts he calmed down and stepped back away from the detective. He sat back on the couch, wiped the saliva from his chin and then rubbed his glasses with his shirttail, muttering obscenities under his breath. Jodie distanced herself from Graham. She stood up and stepped away from him. A police officer picked up the ring from the floor and looked first at Jodie and then at Graham, before deciding to place the ring on the table.

"Is Lucy the poor girl that was attacked?" shivered Jodie through her tears as she looked down at Graham.

He was rubbing his thigh and scowling. He was obviously uncomfortable and potentially volatile. Thompson weighed up the situation with his professional judgement and prepared himself mentally for any confrontation that may arise. He adjusted his posture in preparation of defending the two women and his fellow officers.

"Yes she is, Miss," replied the detective.

Jodie instinctively reached out for a hug. Helen instinctively took it. The two confused and emotionally overwhelmed women embraced in tears and consoled each other. The two uniformed officers and the detective loomed over Graham, who looked up at them through smeared glasses. He had returned to his mild mannered self, which seemed slightly odd to Helen that one man could have such extreme temperaments. He apologised continuously to Helen and Jodie as he began to weep. Jodie and Helen started to walk away slowly.

"Jodie…" he pleaded.

She shook her head without looking back.

Thompson waited as the two women walked out of earshot. He looked on as they supported each other, arms draped across shoulders and their heads tilted onto one and others'. He dropped his line of sight down Jodie's spine, following her contours and the swaying movement of her gait, all the way down to her ankles before taking a deep inhalation through his nose, and exhaled with an audible blow. He hated Graham right now and he knew it would cloud his judgement. If these feelings were reeling through any one of his staff, he would insist they were taken off the case, but he could not do it to himself. Instead, he wiped his forehead with his hand, gathered his thoughts and he sat opposite Graham.

"Now … about this golf course bullshit?" he stared directly at him.

Graham fumbled for words; he opened his hands, shook his head and shrugged his shoulders. He pushed his glasses further up on his nose and rubbed his chin before looking back to the detective.

"I used the golf as a cover. I've been seeing another woman. She's married so I don't want her named, and I'd prefer if Jodie didn't find out too," he looked at the detective with a pathetic, sad dog kind of look. He realised the detective was unmoved by the expression and dropped his gaze to the floor.

"I don't want to hurt her," he shook his head as he started to weep, "You've seen her, she's beautiful, and so caring."

Graham looked up at the detective and stared attentively into his eyes. Could he see that he had hit a nerve? Could he use this against him?

"You make me sick!" the detective stood up and turned away, "You deserve to lose her!"

The uniformed officers followed after him and exchanged opinions as they left.

Graham slunk back into the couch and ran his hand through his hair with a long exhalation of relief. He shuffled slightly and rubbed his thigh in a comforting gesture. After staring at it for some time, he retrieved the ring and slipped it in his trouser pocket.

Helen ushered Jodie into the office behind reception and pressed the button on the coffee percolator. As the system began to bubble and pop, the two women sat on opposite seats and began to talk. Jodie asked about Lucy. What was she like? What did she do? How well did Helen know her? Was she pretty? Helen answered all of her questions as honestly and openly as she could, although she felt incredibly uncomfortable. The two women talked as if they were detached from the whole scenario, as if Helen, Lucy and Jodie were somebody else entirely. They never mentioned Graham at all. When the conversation was as empty as the coffee cups, Jodie straightened herself up and began to leave. She had cried as much as she possibly could and had decided that enough was enough. Her questioning had opened more wounds that it had healed. Helen showed her through to the staff room and offered her the use of the washing facilities and towels. Helen made her polite goodbyes and left Jodie to her thoughts in the wash room. As Helen disappeared back to work, Jodie stared at herself in the mirror. She leaned forward to get eye-to-eye and stared deep into her own red-rimmed reflection. How she wished she could sit with her Aunt and clear all of this heartache out of her stupid little mind.

* * * * *

The working routine had changed dramatically throughout the day which had been very well observed by Tom, who had become frustrated and angry that Helen was not running on time and his day had been drastically altered.

"What the hell's going on, Helen?" he demanded.

"No Tom, not now. Honestly, if I start I won't stop and I need to think before I speak to you. I'm sorry but that's how it is," she stated without making eye contact.

“Serious then?” he almost whispered as Helen turned to leave the room.

The door had barely made contact with the frame before Helen burst back in and threw the door wide open with speed. She was red faced and tear stained. She walked straight over to the foot of Tom’s bed and shouted down at him. Tom looked up at the larger more direct Helen. She stood tall and broad and filled the room with fear and frustration. The red shadows had grown all around her and the icy claws had begun to scratch their way into his mind again. She explained all about Elsie going missing and Lucy being attacked. She told of how she just had to explain to Jodie how wonderful the ‘other woman’ actually was and how uncomfortable that encounter had been.

Tom listened in silence. Helen’s tone and stature, coupled with his own anxiety, had scared him into doing nothing but. She barked on about the events that he had told her and how she felt frightened, of the file she had collated and taken to the police. As she vented her anger, she paced back and forth across the room, waving her arms. The more she explained, the more her anger died down in her manner as it was being released slowly but surely in a shower of explanation and gesticulation. She slowed her speech, she slowed her pace. Eventually, all became still. Her red face lessened and her voice became calm and recognisable again. Unnoticed by both Tom and Helen, she had been weeping and her cheeks glistened in the fading light.

Tom trembled slowly back into his pillows and pulled the sheets up around his chest. He felt nervous but did not recognise it as such; he thought he was cold and excited. He felt like smiling but he knew Helen would not understand. They both took a moment to savour the hushed ambience and reflect on what had been said, most of which filtered through their minds now like echoing reflections of pent up unease diminishing like ripples on a pond. Following a deep breath and an adjustment of his posture, Tom spoke first.

“I had to tell you my secrets Helen, I thought I could trust you with them,” he spoke in a quiet tone, almost apologetically, “you see, I have these attacks, like … anxiety attacks I suppose … panic, you know …" he struggled to catch the words he needed.

"And how do you think I feel? I couldn't …" Helen started,

"I need to rest in peace when my time comes you see, Helen," he interrupted her as if she wasn't even speaking, "having a long life was never one of my plans. I was hoping it would all be over a long time ago but it just never happened. I was hoping that my wayward life would have me in my grave long before now so I wouldn't have to face all this. I did a lot of terrible things in my youth and I did not regret them one little bit for a long time, although something inside me suggested I should. After all these years, my actions have become a cancer to me, eating away at me, destroying me. I thought I could keep it all down. Keep it all hidden but no – my mind is stronger than I am. It controls me, not the other way round."

His voice rose in anger and he shook his fist again.

"I've never held back, I've never felt the need to deny myself the things I desired!" he sounded dark and low, "I went through life admiring women, loving them, they are goddesses and I am their god! But they couldn't see it. They should have given in to me; just come to me of their own accord but I was not blessed with such an attractive magic. I saw beautiful girls with ignorant, arrogant men and it made me wonder why they were not with me!" he shook his fist and scrunched his face, "So I took them, whether they wanted me or not!"

He shook his head to one side and closed his eyes. Helen was in tears. She didn't know what to think. She stood at the side of the bed and trembled.

"You saw the papers; you read the stories. That was me!" he sounded proud and punched his chest, "I evaded the law! I did what I wanted to and nobody stopped me!"

Helen fell into the chair and sobbed with her hands covering the lower half of her face. The pins and needles in her arms and legs were so powerful they made it impossible for her stand, let alone walk. She was trapped.

"They got somebody though, even with DNA they got somebody! Bloody fools! They arrested the wrong man! It wasn't him, it was me!" he shouted, "And that cheeky bastard took MY credit!" he spat through clenched teeth, almost crying in anger.

He remained clenched for a moment and Helen felt tingles of fear running up and down her spine. She felt warmth wrapped all around her, although it was uncomfortable warmth that almost stifled her breathing and crushed her spirit in a vice-like grip.

"I never dreamed I'd get bored of it but I did. I just stopped doing it. I never made an effort to quit - I just stopped!"

He stated very matter of fact, emphasising words to make the point. Then, like a sudden change in the weather, he became the calm after his storm.

"But then, long after, when I met this particular young woman, my thirst became unquenchable. She rekindled my desire all over again. Oh, I loved her for that. Truly loved her with my heart and soul; but you wouldn't understand a feeling of that magnitude would you, Helen? She brought me back. She made me feel so ALIVE again!" he shouted and waved both fists in a victory cheer.

"She was stunning!" he shook his head slowly, half laughing, half-smiling and obviously imagining.

"She was tall and thin, jet black hair and olive skin. Beautiful, beautiful Claire!" he spoke with pauses and smiles, almost poetic, the mood in his voice had changed so dramatically. Helen's head was empty, void of thought and her body was as numb as lead.

"She had just moved into a house on a new estate just outside of town. Her and her boyfriend – who by the way was an ignoramus and did not understand how honoured he was to have her! They wanted to convert the loft into a small bedroom. I said I'd help, as I had the skills. I said I would have to go round there to have a look. It was a simple enough job. The dormer-window had been fitted already. All that was needed was the floorboards and the wall at the end plastered over. I started with the floor and got half of it done that same day. She was very pleased; he was ignorant as usual and quite unsociable with me. He was always angry with her."

He frowned and shook his head. Helen could not believe what was happening, it was all too much. She wished she could switch off right there and then, just end everything and have it all forgotten.

"Anyway… I got back the next weekend and went up to the attic. Turned out her boyfriend had already put a bed and bits and pieces up there. Bloody fool! They'd been arguing and he thought he'd sleep up there as a punishment to her! HA! She thought it was a good thing, a bit of relief; she told me but she didn't tell him! Made it awkward for me though, I had to work round the furniture."

He picked up the sheet and threw it back revealing his feet, which he swung round onto the edge of the bed. He took a minute to comfy himself and then looked up at the ceiling for a moment. Helen felt her hair on the back of her neck prickle and her stomach turned over as she realised he had blocked her escape route. She felt light as a feather yet unable to move. He sat with his feet hovering slightly off the ground as he wriggled his toes.

"I fancied a cup of tea so I went down to the kitchen," he started to swing his legs over the side of the bed in pendulum manner.

"When I got to the bottom of the stairs, I could hear him arguing with her again, calling her names and getting vicious. He made me so angry! I walked up behind him and when he turned around and swore at me, I swung for him," he spoke through his teeth now, "and he flew through the air and onto the floor!"

There was an uncomfortable silence that tormented Helen and tortured her with indecision. She was unsure whether to speak out, leave the room, or stay put. She pondered on the decisions but could muster neither the strength nor the courage to move.

"And Claire screamed at me. The ungrateful bitch actually screamed at me!" he said in a surprised tone as he threw his hands up into the air in front of him. Helen flinched.

"I thought she might have been grateful but what did I know? He was out cold on the floor and she had started crying and screaming, making a terrible noise. I hit her too, and she joined him on the floor. I finished my cup of tea and washed the cup, stepped over them both to reach the sink I did!" he laughed.

"I remember the way she had fallen," he stared at the ground, pointing at where they would be if they were laid in the room with him, "her skirt had risen above the knee and her top had come off her shoulder. She was beautiful. I watched her for a while but then he started to come round. I hit him again, just to be sure, and then I picked him up and put him over my shoulder. I carried him upstairs to the attic. He banged his head on the walls and door frames on the way up, and by the time I sat him in the chair by the dressing table, he was bleeding down one side of his face. He was bobbing his head and murmuring a bit. I hit him again."

He shuffled back into his pillows, swung his legs round and rolled his shoulders as he pulled the sheets up around his waist. Helen breathed a silent sigh of relief and felt slightly less cold. She rubbed her hands together in an attempt to reduce the sweating and twitched her feet rapidly in the hope of gaining some circulation to aid her escape.

"I went back downstairs to see Claire, but she had gone. I looked around and then heard the toilet flushing. I waited for her right outside the toilet door and intercepted her as she came out. She screamed, as I thought she would so I pressed my hand over her mouth. I tried to reason with her, but she was frantic. I had to hold on tight to her skinny little waist and she wriggled all over, waving her arms about. I remember that turned me on – her body wriggling against mine, her fighting like that!" he paused with a smile.

"I carried her upstairs as well. I was only trying to help but she wouldn't have it. She was scratching me and pulling my hair. I gave up pleading in the end and took her into the attic. I grabbed some tape from the toolbox and threw her down on the bed. You know that thick black stuff, the strong stuff? I used that. It was a struggle but I managed to gag her mouth and tape her hands together. She didn't half fight! That turned me on too!"

"When she kicked out at me I taped her feet together. But now he was coming round again! What was I to do? I was caught this time for sure – that's what I thought."

He rubbed his hands together, smiled an evil little smile and nodded his head.

"I grabbed the nail gun from the floor at the end of the bed and shot him through the thigh. He screamed, obviously, so I shot him through the other thigh too! He stopped screaming, but started blubbering and making crying weepy sounds. He reached out to grab me, but he couldn't get up because the nails had gone right through – he was nailed to the chair!" he laughed and clapped.

"What a brilliant idea! I grabbed his arm and nailed that to the chair too. It was bleeding more than I thought. She was shivering and wriggling on the bed, trying to get up. These two were a right handful between them, I can tell you!" he was nodding as he spoke with his eyes open wild.

Helen was shaking her head slowly from side to side as she cried, still frozen to the chair, unable to move and unable to block out the sound of his voice. The fear of nails through her own arms and legs had pinned her down.

"I tied her hands to the head of the bed and the ideas just kept coming. I tied her feet down too, then I held onto her nose, pinched it closed, and held her mouth shut with my palm over the tape until she fell silent. She struggled of course, but eventually, she passed out and lay there, all beautiful and limp."

"He was crying like a baby, his face was just a wet … snotty … bloody … mess. He was trying to pull his arm off the chair with the other arm but couldn't bring himself to do it. It must have hurt!" Tom rubbed his arm as he remembered the scene.

"I grabbed the other hand and nailed that to the chair as well. I rather liked shooting that nail gun and the feeling of the nail punching through the flesh and bone. It was a beautifully muted sound, so wet and warm. Just to be sure that he was definitely not getting up, I nailed his feet to the nice new floor."

He reached out for his tea and took a sip. Helen swallowed hard and rubbed her eyes. She was shaking all over. She felt dizzy and nauseous. Over and over in her mind she was screaming, wishing her legs had the strength to get her away from him and the nightmare he painted in horrifically animated colour. She passed the point of revulsion; the story had become so abstract it could shock her no more. Like the highest point of a terrifying roller coaster, she had reached her apex of fear and she surrendered herself to its ice-cold grip.

"You're safe, Helen," he said sincerely, "I don't do these sorts of things now you know. Couldn't if I wanted to, and to be honest, I have wanted to. Occasionally," he nodded to himself.

"I've often dreamed of you. I taste you in my sleep but I would never hurt you. Not you, Helen. Your friend was nothing to do with me either! I couldn't possibly at my age, in my state!" he laughed, "I bet she tasted good though! I bet she felt wonderful writhing beneath that lucky man!" his voice was slow and sour.

"Anyway… where was I…? Oh yes, I had nailed him and tied her; that's right. I sat on the end of the bed, looking at him. He looked so pathetic, weeping and useless. I went to the bathroom and brought back a flannel to wipe his face. I cleaned him up a bit and he just spat at me, still crying. Ungrateful little bastard! I shot another nail through his arm just to make a point. I sat on the end of the bed. Claire was there, on the bed, tied up and quietly sleeping. She looked so peaceful," he paused and looked thoughtful.

"I love the way she looked, with her arms and legs taped to the corners of the bed. She looked more beautiful than ever. She made me so horny I wanked over her. It didn't take long because I was so wound up and there was so much muck! It sprayed all over her chest, neck and face!"

"I went downstairs to their bedroom and looked through his bedside drawer. I found what I was looking for – condoms. There must have been a dozen or more in there. I told him what I was going to do to her. That I was going to make love to her with feeling, become involved with her body and worship her femininity. He just said 'No' over and over again, cried a lot and closed his eyes. I told him he had to look. He had to be taught a lesson, but he kept his eyes closed. I wanted him to see how she should be treated. I took out a carpet knife from the toolbox and showed it to him."

Tom turned and stared at Helen as he mimed the action of holding a knife. Helen became locked onto the stare almost hypnotically, and braced herself.

"I grabbed his chin and forced his head back so I could get a clear cut. He wriggled a lot and screamed, but I got his eyelid off in the end. It did tear a bit down his cheek, but then he was moving his head around a lot and the blade wasn't as sharp as it could have been. I got the other eyelid a whole lot easier because he was fighting less."

Helen tried very hard not to be sick, repeatedly swallowing her own bile. Her head swayed on her shoulders like a child's toy.

"He had to watch now didn't he? Claire was coming round. I took the knife and opened up her clothes. She was murmuring and shuffling until she came round properly and then she screamed from behind the gag. She sounded muffled, and that sounded sexy to me! I looked at her for a long time, savouring the sights of her magnificent body. She stared back at me with frightened eyes, and that turned me on again."

He turned to Helen and looked sincere, "Have you ever really wanted someone so much you wanted to ... eat them ... absorb them? I mean, somehow ingest their very being?" he shook his head as he struggled to find his words.

Helen was aghast with her head spinning as the images and the words floated violently around in her mind, hurting, provoking and taunting.

"I fell forward and licked her first, like a thirsty dog. I did it right, paid special attention to the clitoris but the ungrateful bitch was still wriggling and trying to escape. I played with her for a while, licking her, kissing her, toying with her. I stroked her body all over, nice and gentle. I made love to her so lightly. I took my time. Kept going back for more as soon as I could after finishing each load and disposing of the condom. I stopped when she became too messy to enjoy. She was red-raw and bleeding. The condoms kept slipping off and I nearly lost one inside her. She didn't like it when I had to feel my way around to get it back."

"She had fainted at some point and was out cold again. He was there in the chair, staring at me, trying to scream, bleeding and weeping and getting slumpier by the minute. His pathetic screams had faded to sobs and he eventually lost consciousness. Then I noticed all the blood that he'd lost. He must have been running on empty for a while, there was loads of it on the floor."

He shook his head and looked down in disbelief.

"I went to the bathroom and cleaned myself up. I got a shower actually! I made sure the condoms were flushed away. Took ages to get the little buggers to disappear down the toilet! I found some of his clothes in their bedroom. I put my clothes in a black bag and took them with me. I packed away the tools, including the nail gun, which wasn't even mine, and took them away too. I cleared up a bit around the hallway and the stairs and went downstairs with my stuff."

"The back door had been open all the time! I couldn't believe it. It was only in the silence downstairs that I had realised just how loud everything must have been upstairs. I was so scared of getting caught. I can't believe I didn't!" he said almost breathless.

"I retraced my steps through the house, back upstairs, double-checking everything. I made up a bucket of salty water to take with me. I don't know why but I thought it was a good idea. I saw it on a film once. I soaked him with the water, poured it over his head. Got another bucket full and washed her nice and slow. She kept flinching and biting her lip. She stared at me, not crying, not screaming, not doing anything really. Just staring at me. She was getting cold so I covered her up. She was asleep when I left."

He paused for a while, tried to sit up but couldn't get a purchase on the bed to push against. He looked over to Helen, who sat shaking and crying then slumped back into his pillows.

"A young man was found hanging around and was arrested. Apparently, he'd been seen going back to the house afterwards. They didn't seem to do any further investigation at all. They never questioned anyone else."

He fell silent, rested his chin on his chest and tilted his head slightly to the left. Helen cried in silence as tears ran down her face.

"Adam Wright," she whispered, "It was your son Adam they arrested."

* * * * *

PC Davis and the maintenance team had returned to search the remaining sections of the huge basement after the fruitless search yesterday. The officer was complaining that the air smelled dank and musty, but the maintenance team, being accustomed to it, could smell nothing. They tutted at each other and gestured in the direction of the PC whenever he moaned about the smell or the dirt. They laughed and joked harmlessly at his inexperience and avoidance of anything that might dirty his uniform. They travelled for what seemed like miles following bundles of pipes across the ceilings and ducking through service hatches into smaller tunnels. The basement was on two levels, separated by flights of concrete stairs. They were looking through the endless corridors and small alcoves of the lower basement when the police officer stopped in his tracks and covered his mouth with the back of his hand.

"Don't tell me you can't smell that?" he said with a disgusted look on his face.

"Yes I can," said Mick, "and that ain't right."

They followed the smell through to a small room at the foot of the lift shafts. The officer reached out to flick on the light but the lonely click was met with no response. In the darkness, the officer clicked the switch up and down a couple more times, as if it would make the light bulb suddenly spring back to life somehow. Giving up on the fruitless exercise, the officer reached into his utility belt and pulled out a torch, the maintenance team did the same from their tool belts. In the collective beams of light flashing across the floor and along the walls, they entered the room and they could see there was a locked metal cupboard in the corner with a dented door.

"Is that one of your storage cupboards?" asked the officer.

Mick just shook his head and shrugged his shoulders.

"It's an old one, hasn't been used for ages, but that isn't," he pointed to the shiny padlock.

They walked into the room and the odour stuck to their noses and throats like tar. They could see in the circular lights of the torches that there was a large dark puddle at the base of the cupboard that reflected the light. The officer reached forward to the padlock to have a closer look. Mick called back to one of his colleagues, standing in the door,

"Fetch us some 'crops, will you, Digger?"

The colleague vanished for a few minutes and after a distant sound of metal creaking and banging, returned with a small pair of bolt croppers. In an instant the padlock was cut and removed from its catch. The cupboard fell open quickly with a loud squeak that echoed through the thin metal casing. Not immediately recognisable, the battered and bloodied body of an elderly woman fell out onto the floor in front of them. Dozens of flies filled the air. Mick turned to be sick in the corner. The vomit sprayed out through his fingers as he tried to cover his mouth to stop it coming out. His colleague at the door turned away as he held his stomach. The officer stared in horror at the mess of congealed blood and hair that was once a face. Her clothes were torn to the point of being almost unrecognisable and her flesh had been lacerated countless times. The blood and material had combined into a soft coating of foul smelling slime.

"We've found her!" said the officer into his radio.

* * * * *

Jodie sat at home in the near darkness of her living room lit only by the flickering of the television screen. She stared blankly at the film, not really watching it but just looking at it;

she did not know what the film was about, nor did she recognise any of the characters or understand the story. Her mind was full of thoughts about Graham, Lucy and Elsie. She slowly got up and walked through to the kitchen, haunted by thoughts of him out with Lucy in the restaurant having dinner, watching them in her mind's eye. They were laughing at her and talking dirty with each other as they kissed and she touched him in ways only Jodie should have done. Her mind flew back to the nights he had spent away from home on the pretence of being with friends. She remembered her conversation with Helen, how Lucy had told her that she was on a first date and realised he must have been seeing other women over the years. He would have brought her fragrance home on his clothes; her flesh would have been touching his. She imagined him thinking of someone else as he made love to her. Jodie felt repulsed. They could have been laughing at her, talking about her, teasing her. Inside she boiled, became hot and twisted and raged with fury. She looked at the various photographs of her and Graham that she had on the fridge door.

Happier times, she thought, when she didn't know about the other women. How could someone so clumsy and ordinary be attractive to other women? Fast and furious thoughts flew through her mind quicker than she could pay them attention. How badly had she been treated? She couldn't tell, but she knew without realising it that if she added up the times that he had had the opportunity to be unfaithful she would be devastated. And how far back dare she think? She felt so foolish and used as she made herself a cup of tea. She paused with the fridge door handle in her hand as she carried the milk, looking at all those colourful pictures again. She felt herself well up inside as tears built up behind her eyes and hot flushes flowed through her cheeks. Her eyes flitted from one image to another as her mind recited the dates and places of each and every happy memory in full glorious colour. Like a dam about to burst, she could feel the inevitable breakdown coming and she was powerless to stop it.

She dropped the milk onto the floor and the contents of the bottle splashed with force across the carpet tiles. She pulled wildly at the pictures. The decorative fridge magnets popped off and bounced across the floor after the milk. She tore at the photographs as she ripped them into strips and threw them up into the air before they too joined the growing white puddle, which still glugged out of the open bottle. She muffled her screams behind gritted teeth and swore as her anger increased with every picture she destroyed. When she had run out of happy memories to desecrate, she grabbed at the fridge. She clawed at the door and pushed against the cold, white metal, rocking the fridge back and forth. Bottles clattered and jostled against each other inside. When the door flew open unexpectedly, she calmed down and stood breathing heavily. She stared through her tears at the mess around her feet. The milk had soaked through her socks and wetted between her toes. The puddle laid across the tiles like a miniature white lake with photographic pleasure boats bobbing across the surface. There looked to be so much milk, more on the floor than she expected to find in one bottle. She looked at the torn smiling faces staring up at her, their emotion unshaken by their recent departure on the not-so-pleasant cruise. They still looked happy in their colourfulness. They still hugged each other as if nothing else mattered. They still had bright faces and love in their eyes. Jodie stared at the debris; all around the silence embraced her in her own private hell. She felt claustrophobic and void of all happiness. Suddenly, the spell was broken by the sound of the back door being pushed open behind her.

"Hi honey I'm home!" he whispered in a sinister tone from over her shoulder.

A razor sharp sensation at the base of Jodie's back made her take a swift intake of breath, though try as she might, she could not exhale. She was choked by the pain of her trapped breath. A second searing sensation shot through her spine and burned up through her chest. Panic welled in her mind as pressure built up inside her. The warmth grew in the small of her back as she felt her life drain slowly from her body. She could not breathe. Her blouse became sodden and heavy; her vision began to blur, her insides started to burn. She felt her legs get weak and she fell to her knees. Not having the strength to keep her balance, she fell forward face first, and splashed into the milk as her rich red blood turned the white puddle pink.

* * * * *

Helen found herself all cried out, laid in a steaming hot bath. She tried hard to relax and let the aroma of the bubbles 'ease her troubled mind', as promised on the label and in their long-running advertising campaign, but to no avail. She washed herself slowly in silence, lingered as she stroked her skin with her soft sponge, squeezing the foam over her, running in streams into the water all around. Her skin had reddened with the heat by the time she got out and she felt slightly dizzy. She walked through to her bedroom slowly, holding on to the wall for support. She took a towel from the cupboard and wrapped it around her hair. She took her bathrobe off the peg on the back of her bedroom door and tied it tightly around her as she steadily made her way down stairs.

She walked into the kitchen, leaned up against the worktop and contemplated making a cup of tea. She visualised the motions; filling the kettle, getting the milk, and decided that she just wanted a rest and wished someone else could do it for her. Where was Nathan when she really needed him? She looked into the kitchen window, with the light of the room and the darkness outside she could see her reflection clearly. She removed the loose towel from her head, bent forward and wrapped her long, wet hair into it. She stood up and looked at her reflection again to check the towel was straight. Just then, she saw something outside in the shadows; a twinkle of something bright in the darkness of the garden. She reached out to the wall and flicked the light off. With the light out the reflection had vanished from the window and she could see that somebody was out there, lurking in the bushes along the side of her garden. A black figure was clearly visible against the skyline. Her fear rose, almost to the point of despair as she questioned again and again, "why me?"

She staggered across the kitchen and made her way towards the phone on the far wall. She felt cold, alone and scared. She took hold of the phone so tightly that her knuckles turned white in her grip as she slowly raised it to her ear. She looked out into the garden but could see nothing. Suddenly, the door behind her opened and she screamed. She dropped the handset and fell back against the wall.

"Its OK, just me..." said Nathan.

He stood in the kitchen doorway with both hands out in front of him, palms down. Helen cried as she slumped down the wall and onto the floor.

"There's somebody outside," she whispered, shivering.

Nathan went over to the window and looked out.

"I can't see anyone," he said reassuringly.

He went out through the back door and into the garden.

"No!" screamed Helen, short and sharp, but he had already gone.

Helen was alone again. The sounds of the night amplified in her ears as dark imaginings and whispering voices invaded her terrified mind. She moved slowly, trying to see into the garden, not wanting to get too near to the open door for fear of someone jumping out at her. Nathan appeared suddenly from the darkness. His black clothes provided an excellent camouflage against the backdrop of the night. Helen shivered uncontrollably, fell back against the wall and returned to the floor. She began to sweat and her lips quivered. He sat next to her, grumbling as he lowered himself, and put an arm around her. He rubbed his thigh with the other hand.

"Nobody there, love, nobody there. It's OK," he whispered reassuringly.

Helen worried to herself and did not feel safe. Something inside told her something was wrong and her fear was rising at an alarming rate. Nathan looked her in the eye as he had never done before and nodded slowly.

"It's all right. I'm home now," he said slowly.

Helen trembled and opened her mouth. Nathan stroked her arm with true tenderness and kissed her on the cheek.

"It's OK. Calm down. Nobody there."

He groaned a little in his throat and rubbed his thigh again. Helen started to calm down and her fear diminished slowly.

"You OK? What's up with your leg?" she asked.

"It's OK, just a squash injury," came the reply.

"And you smell of perfume!" Helen got up fast and looked down at Nathan, and then she flinched as she remembered the stranger outside and looked out of the window. Her startled reflection was all that stared back at her.

"It's not what you think! The lads were messing about in the changing rooms. You know what they're like!" he tried to get up and winced.

He held out a hand for Helen to help him. She looked at him, shook her head, turned and left the room. She slammed the door behind her.

"Bitch!" whispered Nathan under his breath as he struggled to his feet.

TUESDAY

Helen felt as if her ears were full of warm cotton wool and her throat had become tight. She had been sick first thing in the morning and put it down to nerves after the incident last night. Before going to bed she had phoned the police to report the sighting but as she had no description and Nathan had found nothing in the garden, the police were taking no further action. The officer stated that a squad car would search the area and her sighting would be recorded. She given a special hotline number and reminded that she should call them again if she saw anything else. Helen guessed by the tone of his voice that he had cited that well-rehearsed script several times over the past few weeks. She was finding it hard to focus on her morning routine and kept pausing, seemingly at random, to stare blankly into the middle distance. Nathan had not come up to bed last night and she was surprised to find the couch empty, though she was not as angry as she thought she would be. It looked like he had left at some time during the night as there were no breakfast pots scattered across the worktop in the kitchen, as was the usual indication that Nathan had been there. She had considered taking the day off but thought that being occupied would help her keep her mind off things and if she stayed home she would have dwelled on matters and made herself feel worse. As a matter of comfort, she phoned to book another session with Lynn to address her emotions before leaving the house. The drive to work was a silent one; a silence broken only by thought. The roads were almost clear and the traffic lights were in her favour. The lack of heated exchanges and jostling on the roads made Helen feel a little easier and she started to relax although the delicate shade of nausea still haunted her from within.

When she noticed the time she realised she was more than an hour early and that would explain why the roads were so clear. Once at work she felt slightly better than when she left the house. She breezed in and out of the staff room and was ready to go in an instant. With only polite hellos to her colleagues, she remained task-focussed and did not stop for small talk. She had some time before her appointment and decided she would begin her rounds after she had taken a refreshing stroll around the gardens. Walking slowly she admired the shrubs and the sound of the birds in the trees all around her. Such a wonderful, clear, enlightening place, she thought, how could it have been desecrated by the attack of such a beautiful young woman? The dark shadow of the unpleasant thought crept into her mind and raised elements of her fears. She scurried in through the main entrance as if the outside world would grab her from behind if she was too slow. Inside, among colleagues and friendly faces, she began to relax again and started on her rounds. Hesitantly, cautiously, she walked up to Tom's door, determined not to let him burden her with any more stories and not to let him see that she was buckling from the weight he had passed onto her. She breathed deeply and reached for the door handle. Just before she took hold of it, she dropped her hand, rubbed her face and breathed deeply again. She reached out for the handle and squeezed so hard her hand became warm and paled at the creases. The warm cotton wool feeling built up in her ears again. She paused, and with a short, sharp grunt of frustration, she released her grip on the handle. She walked around in a small circle in the corridor, breathed deeply and wiped her face with her hands, braced herself again, closed her eyes and visualised the picture of St Anthony in the counselling room. She focussed on his pleasant expression to calm her and then pushed open the door. When she opened her eyes again, she saw Tom sleeping silently on his pillows. His eyes were closed and he looked peaceful. How could such a harmless old man cause so much distress? Helen tilted her head and smiled a small smile, drawn by the softness and charm of old man Tom, like a cute puppy in the pet shop. Her feelings and thoughts played tug-of-war though she was determined to remain professional and carry out her duties. She forced herself to speak.

"Happy Birthday Tom," she said quietly as she walked over and pulled the table across his bed.

He didn't move. There was no reaction at all. Instinctively, Helen knew what was wrong. She reached out and put the back of her hand against his cheek. He was cold. She stood motionless for a moment then placed the tray on the table before she pulled the table away from the bed.

"Goodbye Tom," she whispered as she left the room.

Helen walked down to reception and told Marie that she had found Tom dead in his bed. Both women had been through this routine a dozen times or more but neither of them had become accustomed to the experience. There was always a sense of sadness and loss, even now, even for this monster. Perhaps this was similar to Tom's respect for those young drug addicted thieves, she wondered. Marie was very solemn and quiet as she made three mandatory phone calls. As the two women stood in silence, Marie took a pad from a file and completed a pre-printed form. She removed the top copy and filed the pad back in its original place. Helen leaned up against the desk in the reception area as she waited for the manager and the doctor. The pair arrived with synchronised strides, almost militaristic, marching towards the waiting women. The doctor approached the reception with his hand outstretched and Marie offered the paperwork, which he took without breaking his stride.

The four of them went down to Tom's room and the doctor read the page as he walked. Helen led the way as Marie walked behind, rushing her pace to keep up with the quick-stepping doctor. She unfeelingly informed the manager of who Tom was and a brief history of his time in St Anthony's as they marched. When they arrived at the room, Helen knocked out of habit. The manager brushed past her and opened the door, shaking his head. The doctor went over to the bed, checked for a pulse and looked over the body for any obvious marks while the manager watched from the back of the room.

The voice of the doctor did not register with Helen; she heard only muffled sounds as she saw his mouth moving but the two were very separate, like a badly dubbed film. The room became a carousel spinning round, rising and falling. Dizziness engulfed Helen. She felt empty and her legs gave way. Something hit the back of her head as the floor embraced her and brought the spinning to a halt.

She found herself standing in a large marshland surrounded by thick green foliage with wisps of steam emanating from beneath. The only sound was that of old crows, crawing through the still, humid air. She could smell the dampness of the earth and the stagnant water. She stood silent, trying to scream out loud but making no sound, her long lace robes blew in slow motion in the non-existent breeze. She looked at her hands and stared in awe as her flesh moved like the black and white fizzing of an old television screen lacking a reception. She looked over to the horizon in time to see a figure floating towards her. It was a man, an old man, in a long brown robe. When he neared her, she could see it was St Anthony, smiling gently with his golden halo fading into the distance. Helen began to feel relieved. He landed silently on his feet a few yards away from Helen and walked slowly over the green tufts of marsh grass towards her. He was smiling with gentle eyes. The greenery around his feet faded to ash with every step. Helen felt somewhat unnerved as his face faded to a blank, featureless oval, his hair became like fire and raged red and yellow. It flickered into the sky and sent rainbows flying like fireworks before they exploded into stars across the clouding heavens. He raised his arms out to his sides, his robe filling the space like giant batwings to reveal his two companions within the folds. The old lady appeared to have her eyes closed and held a bloodstained knife out to Helen. The blade had cut into her fingers and the red streams trickled down her arm before dripping slowly from her elbow. On closer inspection, Helen saw that her eyes had been cut from their sockets and only the dark, blood-stained hollows remained. The young boy was crying and carrying a lamb with its throat cut; the blood had congealed and matted the wool. Suddenly, the old lady, the young boy and the lamb turned and screamed towards her; their faces increased in size to cover her entire field of vision. Their open mouths filled with rows upon rows of razor sharp teeth as their features smoothed into their flesh and became void of life. She turned to run and found that Tom's face had appeared behind her and was laughing loud and long. He ebbed away into the distance as he spewed golden lions at her. They roared ferociously as they charged towards her, followed by showering rose petals and red hair ribbons, fluttering through the dank air. Suddenly, a giant hand flew in from the side and snatched hold of Helen.

With a jolt she awoke and lay motionless. In a state of mild shock, she stared up at the ceiling waiting for the full impact of reality to settle her down. She was saturated with sweat and she ached all over. She was in Marie's office behind reception, laid on the settee with a cold flannel across her forehead. Still feeling unnerved by the dream, she moved slowly, not wanting to make herself feel any dizzier than she already did. She reached for the flannel and pulled it away. She tossed it on the arm of the settee before moving herself round very carefully and leaned forward with her head in her hands. Marie appeared by her side with a glass of water.

"Drink this Helen, then I'll take you home."

Helen sipped in silence as Marie watched. Helen was a mess of emotion. Tides of sadness, confusion and fear swirled like torrential currents through her system. She felt drained and lifeless. Marie could see that her face was unhealthily pale and her hands were trembling. After the water had gone and Helen had brought herself round to a more responsive state of mind, Marie gave her a lift home. The drive was like a roller coaster in slow motion for Helen. Every turn and every bump in the road seemed exaggerated. Her stomach rolled and her head swam. Marie kept giving sideways glances, to be sure that Helen was OK and that she was not going to be sick in her car. Helen noticed how they hit every red light and every pelican crossing had somebody crossing it. The coincidence was amusing but Helen could hardly muster up the strength to smile, never mind laugh. Eventually, after what seemed an unnecessarily long journey, they turned into Helen's street and pulled up in the only available parking space just a few doors down from Helen's house.

"Shall I walk you up to your door?" offered Marie, tugging back the handbrake.

"No thanks, you get back. I'll be in tomorrow," said Helen with a forced smile.

"No you won't" replied Marie, in a firm tone.

Helen unlocked the door and waved to Marie as she drove away. She pushed the door open with her shoulder as she leaned her weight against it, pulled the key out with a feint struggle and staggered over to the couch. She fell back into the welcoming comfort of the soft furnishings, still wearing her coat and shoes, and lay down across the couch. With her arm across her forehead she meandered her way reluctantly into a deep dark sleep.

* * * * *

He sat alone, upstairs on the back seat of the bus, staring out of the window, watching intently as the pretty young girls in their school uniforms laughed and joked at the bus stop. Bitter resentment, borne of rejection, fuelled his thoughts; they knew that their behaviour and the way they dressed were provocative and they deliberately flaunted themselves for sexual attention. That is all teenage girls ever did; all they have ever done. Even in his own teenage years they provoked and enticed only to dismiss his advances. What gave them the right to tantalise and advertise their bodies yet hold back when it came to the crunch? Children can be so cruel; school girls are even more vicious. The loose tie around their necks beneath opened buttons that revealed flesh above the fresh, young cleavage was enough to make him shiver with joy. They danced in the bus stop as they passed a cigarette round while they flaunted themselves without inhibitions. He watched them circling and chatting, swaying their hips and throwing back their long hair over their soft shoulders.

Seduced into a daydream, he imagined owning a schoolgirl for himself. A naive, gullible girl that he could manipulate into doing anything he desired. Someone he could use and abuse and she wouldn't even know it; he could have her do anything he pleased. He put his hand in his pocket and felt himself; he squeezed and gently massaged his erection. In his private pleasure, he squirmed, rubbing his back against the seat. He was dragged back into reality when his attention was stolen by a long-haired blonde who came down the aisle towards him. She bumped from side to side as the bus pulled away from the stop on its long journey to the nearby villages. Trying hard to remain upright, she hung on to the handrails, laughing as she did so. She smiled and said 'Hello' as she sat clumsily on a seat in front of him to his left. Her swagger coupled with the stale smell of cigarettes and alcohol confirmed his suspicion that she was more than a little drunk and in a good mood to make friends so he smiled back at her and asked her name.

"Lisa," she replied.

"So Lisa, what have you been up to?" he asked calmly.

She told him that she'd been out with her workmates as one of her colleagues was going on maternity leave and they had lunch out to celebrate. He looked her up and down as she spoke. She was wearing a navy blue suit with a flowery shirt and high heeled shoes. Her name badge had "Lisa" written on it above a logo that he didn't recognise.

"So where do you work, Lisa?"

"Travel Wise on Maine Square. You want to go on holiday?" she giggled.

He smiled at her, raised his eyebrows and beckoned her to sit next to him. As she staggered up towards him and sat down with a bump, he shuffled slightly to get closer to her.

"Now you just wash it mishter," she smiled, waving her finger in the air, "I see you looking at me!"

"But you look so good! What else am I supposed to do, Lisa?"

"You wanna see me? You wanna piece of these?" she unbuttoned her blouse and revealed her ample bosom, only just contained in a red lace bra that was obviously too small. Her breasts wobbled as the bus bumped up and down on the road. Slowly, he reached out to touch her and she leaned back quickly, teasingly out of reach.

"No!" she snapped as she pulled her blouse closed, "You could be anyone. How do I know you're not the dreaded Creepy Crawly?" she laughed.

"Oh but I am, Lisa" he replied firmly, "and you're next!"

"You?" she laughed as she took his hand and placed it on her breast, "You're softer than these beauties!"

He squeezed gently, nodded his head and hummed to himself. She slid her hand over his thigh and began to caress his erect penis through the thin material of his trousers.

"Not that soft though, eh?" he smiled.

With a determined look in her eye, she slid herself across as she sat astride him. She kissed him passionately as she pulled his erect penis out of his unzipped trousers and began playing with him. He had his hands pushed up beneath her bra and was caressing her breasts beneath the lace. He gently rubbed the erect nipples with his thumbs before he slipped his hands around her back and unclipped the catch. She felt for the straps inside her sleeves and smiled smugly as she removed her bra without removing her blouse. She dropped it nonchalantly and fell onto him in another passionate kiss. He stroked her flesh as he felt his way up to her neck and the gently over her cheeks. With a firm yet gentle grip, he took hold of her hair and began to push her down towards the floor in front of him.

"I'll never fit down there!" she laughed, looking at the gap between his legs and the seat in front of them.

"Shuffle down, baby, you know you want to."

He pushed her again and shuffled back as far as he could. With a hand on each shoulder, thumbs across her throat, he pushed her down into the space. Although she resisted slightly and found it hard to get comfortable, she did not object and took him in her mouth. He leaned back in the seat with his eyes closed and held onto the sides of her head with both hands as she bobbed up and down. She murmured and hummed as she worked her tongue around him. He gripped her head as he came closer to orgasm, she worked faster and he gripped even harder. She began to make a noise in her throat, like a muffled, burbling scream as he forced her up and down on him, her head at the mercy of his command. The seat behind her rubbed against her back and she wriggled to get clear. He got angry, growled and gritted his teeth as he forced himself down into her throat and made her gag. She tried to escape his grip but she could not get loose; she pushed against his legs but she didn't have the reach to push herself away. Her back was trapped by the seat behind and she could not find a space to move into. She punched his thighs frantically and tried to rock her body from side to side but he had her trapped. In desperation, she tried to bite him but her gag reflex had forced her mouth open and almost locked her jaw wide. He rammed himself into her as he ejaculated, banging her head and pushing himself deeper inside with every expulsion. She felt the warm slime explode into her mouth as he pinched her nose shut. Choking, she immediately began to reach. The bile and alcohol burned deep in her throat. He held the top of her head with his free, outstretched hand and gripped tightly on to her hair. As the bus bounced this way and that she rocked back forth, hitting the seat behind her and then pressing against him. With his thighs pressed hard against her shoulders she was trapped. Ferociously uncaring, he pounded himself violently into her as she choked on her own vomit and his semen, gurgling in the depths of her gullet. The warmth of the fluids excited him further and the scratching of her teeth on his sensitive flesh only fuelled his desire. Her eyes watered and her vision blurred. Starved of oxygen, she began to panic in a pressurised silence. Instinctively, she widened her mouth and took a sharp intake of breath, which served only to lock more mucus and slime in her already clogged throat. With deliberate intent, he forced himself in again, totally blocking her windpipe, and he held himself there. Her mouth closed around him as he held her tight, his testicles pushed hard against her chin. As her consciousness faded, his excitement rose. He gripped her hair in his fist so tight that several strands of it tore out of the scalp as the bus rocked. Her bloodshot eyes were bulging in their sockets and streamed with tears. With the little strength she had left she tried to bite down but to no avail, she gripped his thighs with her outstretched fingers, she twitched uncontrollably as her body went into spasm. Starved of air, she fell still and he held her there loosely. As his arousal subsided he leaned back into the seat and let go of her head. She slumped down on the floor as semen and vomit trickled from the corner of her mouth and out of her nose. He quickly reached down, took her under the arms and dragged her up onto the seat beside him. He looked out of the windows and saw that the bus had left town and was travelling through the green belt beyond the suburbs. The terminus was only a few more stops away. He knew he had to alight at this stop or the next in order to avoid discovery.

He leaned her into the corner of the back seat and she slumped against the window. Her head fell forward and her chin rested on her chest allowing another string of slime to escape from her mouth. Smiling to himself, he took hold of her blouse and pulled it wide open to expose her breasts. He paused to admire her welcoming bosom and then pulled her across him with her breasts on his lap. He smeared his moist penis against her flesh, deliberately manipulating the breasts to squeeze his penis in her cleavage, and then he wiped himself clean on her blouse. After he had straightened her lifeless body in the corner again, he tidied her clothes to make it look like she was sleeping. He smiled as he tapped her firmly on the cheek.

"You dirty little slag!" he whispered in her ear before he stood up to leave.

* * * * *

Helen woke up to the sound of giggling and talking coming from outside the front door. She felt stiff and uncomfortable having fallen asleep in an awkward position. To make matters worse, she was still wearing her coat and shoes and they had not helped her circulation as she slept. Rubbing her neck, she sat up slowly and looked out towards the front door. Two people were coming into her house, one of them was a woman and the other was Nathan.

Laughing and joking, the couple burst through the front door together. The woman threw her arms around Nathan's neck and started to kiss him; he took hold of her waist and returned the affection. When Helen appeared at the end of the hall the two were locked in a passionate embrace. Nathan saw her out of the corner of his eye and stopped what he was doing so suddenly that the woman almost fell onto the floor.

"Shit!" he whispered.

She stumbled slightly but managed to level herself out, pull her coat and straighten her skirt. Helen could see and smell that they had both been drinking.

"Who the hell is she?" asked the woman, pointing with her thumb as if hitchhiking.

"Ah…" was Nathan's reply, "Yes…."

"Thanks, Nathan. That's just great!" Helen stormed through to the kitchen.

Lost in the confusion of the situation, Nathan fumbled for words and tried to be as sober as he possibly could, which he found very difficult. He pushed the woman away from him when she tried to latch onto him for another kiss, much to her surprise. The woman protested loudly to Nathan as he ushered her out of the door. He apologised constantly and assured her that he would call her later. The more he pushed her away, the louder and more abusive her resistance became. Helen heard the conversation boiling over from the kitchen and kicked a cupboard door so hard she hurt her foot. She slipped off her shoe to rub her toes then began to take her coat off as she heard the front door close. She was furious. Her face was burning and her hands were sweating. She gathered her thoughts and tried to stop herself shaking.

"Wanker!" shouted the other woman from outside the front door.

"Damn right!" whispered Helen in agreement as she left the kitchen and entered the hallway.

After all she had been through, how could he do this to her? Nathan was swaying slightly with his arms open and a smile on his face.

"Whatsermatter babe?" he slurred.

"You bastard! Get out!" she screamed, storming past Nathan to get to the front door, nudging his shoulder so hard he nearly fell backwards. She had hoped to keep her dignity and not let him see her anger but she fell at the first hurdle. The very sight of him smiling had lit the fuse and now she was ready to explode. Standing in the hallway, she held the door open as she looked down at the floor. Her clenched fist shook beside her, with tight clenched teeth she breathed heavily through her nose. She could feel her heart pounding in her ears. Nathan staggered slowly towards her as he shook his head in disbelief.

"But you're spost to be at work aren't you?"

"Because that would make it all right wouldn't it Nathan? If I wasn't here, you could have had your fun couldn't you? How many times as this happened then?" she shouted, hitting him about the face and head without any real aim or care as to where the blows landed. Nathan ducked and weaved as best he could but he couldn't avoid the numerous impacts. Helen reached out and grabbed his shoulders. She pulled as hard as she could and he fell towards her. With a quick shuffle of balance and a change of her footing, Nathan found himself falling down the steps outside into the street. He lifted his head, wiped his bleeding nose on his sleeve and looked up at Helen, who raised her middle finger to him before she slammed the door.

* * * * *

Thompson stood uneasily at the front of a room full of attentive officers. He rocked back and forth from his heels to his toes, stepping sideways now and again to relieve the strain on his aching feet. The officers about the room took notes and listened keenly. They looked to Thompson with respect. He had worked himself up through the force since leaving school, and for someone of his mixed ethnic background in this small-minded county, it had been a battle worthy of recognition, if not a medal. He had a lot of anger in him, built up from years of racial abuse, which simmered steadily and he released through his work. Even though he had learned how to use his negative feelings in a positive way and successfully battled against years of prejudice, he still found himself incredibly nervous when speaking to a room full of his most trusted colleagues.

On a glass panel at the front of the room were photographs of people and places, drawn together with coloured pens with printed notes beneath them. The detective walked across the front of the display, using a blue laser-pen to draw attention to the relevant pictures as he spoke. He pointed out the victims of the Crawler, stating locations, names, dates and the nature of the attacks. He pulled together as much background on the victims as he had about their families, lifestyles and places of work. As constables and colleagues added important details, he wrote them quickly on the glass beneath the pictures. After a pause to survey the display, he took a step away from the board and leaned forward on a table.

"Now this is an odd one. We have been advised to look into the car incident that happened over the weekend. The Cold Case Team have reason to suspect the Crawler was somehow involved in this. Although there is evidence from the wreckage that the car was indeed sabotaged, there is nothing to suggest that it is linked to the Crawler, but… the CCT have their reasons so we do the legwork."

A groan came from the back of the room, which was quickly followed by an unheard comment. Thompson guessed it was nothing more than an unprofessional moan at another department which had often been seen to interfere with 'real' police work.

"It's what we do people – we find things out! Now… the young woman in the car was Lisa Taylor, 29 years of age, lived alone and worked on the deli counter in her local supermarket. Find out what she did, who she knew, where she was going and why. Ridley and Knights, you take that one," he looked over to two young uniformed officers who nodded back at him.

"As far as we know, none of these victims knew each other. Even the survivors of suspected attacks do not recognise any of these other victims. There is no underlying factor here apart from what we believe to be a convenient time and place," he paused, "that is to say that it may be these women were selected purely because they were in the wrong place at the wrong time, maybe he was just passing, or already in the area. There is nothing to suggest that these women were followed or stalked prior to their attack. All of these women were alone at the time. Ladies and gentlemen, we are dealing with a genuine psychopath, choosing his victims at random for nothing more than his own perverted pleasure!"

He walked forward to the centre of the room and perched on the edge of a desk. All eyes followed him in silence as he bowed his head for a moment and gathered his thoughts in the still ambience before he spoke in a softer tone.

"Sixteen year old Maria Saint was beaten to death in her own home. She was killed and violently sexually assaulted post-mortem. He washed her thoroughly before and after death but we still have DNA. The clothes she had been wearing had been put through the washing machine, along with the unfortunate pet dog! We have the Criminal Psychologist report in the file that I expect every one of you to read. This one's a real sicko people; let's get him off our streets!"

He got up off the table and walked back to the board, picked up a pile of papers and handed them to the officer on the table nearest to him. The officer took the top copy and passed the pile to his colleague who did the same.

"We also have reason to believe, and probable DNA to suggest that the Crawler is somehow related to, or a copy-cat of the Garden Creeper who was active in this area some years ago; check the dates. There are details of associated incidents in the file you have now. This file is recommended for your bedtime reading people, be sure to make yourself familiar with it! OK? Class dismissed!"

He summoned WPC Jordan over to him and her colleague joined them too. They stood at the front of the room by the glass board.

"Will you go over to see Miss Manning? Try and get some background on this Graham Rice character. I think he may cause trouble with Jod … I mean Miss Manning… and Miss Waters. Check her out too. Just make a routine courtesy call will you? Check out her Crawler sighting with her and see if you can get some background on her boyfriend, what's his name?"

"Yes sir, we'll do it."

The two officers took the addresses from the file and turned to leave. Thompson stood with his hands on his hips in the empty room, raising and lowering himself on his toes. He stroked his chin and gazed over the photographs, reading the faces and the tag lines as he tried to make sense of it all. Another officer entered the room holding a file of papers and came over to Thompson.

"Miles? What you got for me?"

"This is the evidence from the old lady in the basement. Estimated time of death is between twelve and three on Saturday afternoon. She was attacked with a three-pronged garden fork. The kind you hold in one hand, the size of a trowel?" he curled three fingers to mimic the fork.

"She was struck approximately thirty-four times across her upper body and nineteen times to her head. It was a vicious attack. None of the wounds were deep enough to kill her and the coroner confirms that she would have bled to death, bearing in mind there is no evidence of heart attack and some of the medication she was taking would have stopped the blood clotting," he paused and stumbled for words, "the coroner also suggests that she was alive when she put into that locker; her fingernails showed that she had tried to scratch her way out. She must have been so weak by then, but she never gave up."

Thompson thumbed through the file as his colleague spoke.

"Where did the initial attack take place?" Thompson asked, not looking up from the file.

"It's looking like the lady was attacked in a room close to the one she was found in. The only reason she was moved, we suspect, is because there was nowhere to hide the body in the first room. She was probably unconscious when she was taken down there, came round and then attacked. We have two teams working on the evidence now, sir."

"Good. Prints? DNA? Suspects?"

"We found the murder weapon with no prints on it, but it did have black wool fibres and a human hair. The hair belongs to the young girl, Maria Saint that was attacked in her home over the weekend. Now that raises the question – why would the Crawler kill an old lady? It doesn't fit his usual MO. There's no sexual motive at all."

"Jesus! What the hell…?" Thompson walked a couple of steps away, stroking his chin, looking at photographs of

Elsie's injuries, taken by the coroner. In amongst the photos were stills from the CCTV. Several stills showed two individuals entering the building within minutes of each other, through different doors.

"That sir is a confirmed sighting of Graham Rice entering the building on the day of the killing but no record of him ever leaving through any of the main entrances, all of which are covered by CCTV."

"We have another unidentified male here," the officer pointed to a second figure in another still, "also seen entering the building on the Saturday without appearing to have left through any of the normal exits. We have been assured that he does not work there," the officer paused for breath.

"He appears to have gained entry through the staff residential quarters, sir. We are checking through husbands and partners now, sir."

Thompson remained silent and still, locked in deep thought.

"We spoke to the maintenance staff on duty at the time of the sighting, sir, and they said they found a window open, just a short distance from where we found the murder weapon. Although it is unusual, they never officially reported it at the time because it didn't seem that important."

* * * * *

The two female officers had no answer from the front door, despite their constant knocking and shouting, and so tried their luck around the back. Through the window, WPC Jordan saw Jodie's body face down on the floor in a pool of what looked like pink paint, drying into the carpet tiles with torn up paper all around. The door was unlocked and the officer hurried in as she talked quickly into her radio, her colleague behind her. Jordan instinctively reached out for Jodie's neck to check her pulse but knew she was dead. She had lost a lot of blood from two deep incisions to her lower back. The murder weapon, a large kitchen knife, was beside her in the strange pink liquid. Jordan noticed a slight movement in her peripheral vision and instinctively looked up through the open door. There, at the foot of the stairs, sat a young boy in his pyjamas, gently weeping as he hugged his teddy bear.

Within minutes a swarm of police officers had circled the house and stretched yellow tape across the front and back gardens. Inevitably, neighbours had gathered and speculated wildly. The area just outside the back garden had been taped off and three police officers had begun to search the lawn and surrounding flowerbeds.

"The murderer walked through the fluid and left three distinct footprints across the carpet into the living room. Looks like he'd been upstairs into the kid's room. Lucky kid!"

One forensic examiner took photographs of the footprints, while another squatted next to Jodie's body and carefully placed the knife in a clear plastic bag. He then began to scrape a sample of the pink fluid onto a spoon and drop it into a small plastic container. He collected some of the paper with colourful stains and dropped them into a bag after holding them up to the light in the tweezers.

"Photo's…" he said quietly, "and this gooey stuff is milk and congealed blood. The bottle is there, she must have dropped it and it leaked all over here. She lost a lot a blood from the stab wounds and hey presto – pink goo!"

DI Thompson went outside to the back garden, ran his fingers through what little hair he had left and sighed loudly. He had seen dead bodies before, but this one had upset him on a personal level. This time he had the additional pressure of being attracted to the dead woman. He closed his eyes and saw flashes of her face, tear-stained and saddened. Before his sadness could grip him, he opened his eyes quickly and looked over at the boy, who was staring back at him with lonely, deeply saddened eyes from the back seat of a patrol car. He dropped his gaze and shook his head slowly. The detective spoke with his colleagues and they were quick to confirm that this was the work of the Crawler, although Thompson knew that already. He was getting nervous, his flesh tingled and his mouth became dry. Wrestling with his emotions, he paced up and down with both hands on the sides of his head, inhaling long and loud. He pushed his hands round to the back of his neck and stretched out with a throaty grunt. Out in the street and beyond the small gathering of neighbours, a car drew slowly closer. Miles got out quickly before it had come to a halt and ducked under the tape. He rushed over to Thompson, who on seeing him in such a hurry had started down the garden to meet him in the street. Almost instantly, a rapid succession of flashes hit his eyes and made him flinch. He put his arm around Miles and they jogged back to the safety of the garden, away from the invasive local media.

"I've found it" Miles began, "Rice's history."

The two walked back into the house and found a quiet corner. Miles handed Thompson a file.

"Adam Wright, the man arrested as the Garden Creeper, was his grandfather. Adam's son, Anthony Wright was placed in hiding as a child for his own protection when his father, the Garden Creeper, was jailed. He was moved out of town and fostered out to another family, protected by Law and changed his name to Rice. He lived safely under that name until he had a family of his own and made the fatal mistake of returning here. Unfortunately for the Rice family, the press somehow found out who they were and exposed them. As a result, the family were victimised by the neighbours. They suffered a long string of violent attacks and hate mail; the kids were assaulted on their way home from school and a relative of one of the Creeper's victim's sexually assaulted Rice's sister in a revenge attack. It was all too much for Anthony and only two months after that assault he shot his daughter and his wife before shooting himself. Graham was shot too though only wounded. He was eleven at the time and witnessed his family massacred by his father."

Thompson thumbed through the file and said nothing.

"There is an alleged history of mental illness in the family. They have a genetic tendency towards personality disorder apparently, or so the family doctor claimed in Adam's defence during the Garden Creeper trial. Graham spent a long time in an institution for research and medication as a kid. They prodded and probed that boy for five long years!"

"Jesus H Christ!" whispered Thompson, shaking his head, "Get all available officers to search for Rice, I want him in custody as soon as!"

WEDNESDAY

Helen had been crying in her sleep and her pillow was still damp when she woke. She had gathered the duvet towards her and hugged it tight with one arm and one leg exposed in the cool air of the bedroom. Desperately seeking safety and warmth, she rolled herself under the duvet and snuggled herself into the deep welcoming folds. She slid across to Nathan's pillow and threw hers on the floor behind her. She inhaled deeply and could smell the feint traces of his aftershave. She punched his pillow as she started to weep. After a long battle trying to restrain her emotional turmoil, she considered herself composed and gathered her thoughts, rolled out of bed and trudged into the bathroom. In silence, she washed and returned to the bedroom to dress. As she stared at herself in her full-length mirror she paid particular attention to the slightly increased size of her tummy and thighs. She turned sideways just to be sure and patted her stomach. A knock at the front door startled her. She grabbed a blouse lazily draped on the back of a chair and stepped off downstairs as she pulled it around her. There was another knock at the door.

"OK, OK, I'm coming," she called as she looked for her keys on the sideboard.

She opened the door and was met by the librarian that had introduced her to the digital media viewers in the library. He opened his mouth to speak but fell silent with his mouth ajar and stared at Helen, practically naked from the waist down.

"Wow!" he gasped.

"What the hell are you doing here? How did you find me?" she quizzed, pulling at her blouse and trying to hide herself from his gaze.

"I got your records from the Library, I know I shouldn't but I had to see you again."

"What…?" Helen pondered for a moment and then reached a quick conclusion, "I'm not a member – you can't have done!"

The young man fumbled and fidgeted.

"OK, OK. I'm sorry. I followed you! I left shortly after you did and followed you here. I had to see you. I wanted to see you then but I didn't have the balls to knock on the door. Since then, I haven't stopped thinking about you. I dream of you. I make love to my girlfriend and I imagine she's you!" he shrugged his shoulders and made a step towards her.

"You can't come in here – my boyfriend will be back any minute!"

"No he won't! You threw him out yesterday, I saw you!" he shook his head and smiled his smug little smile.

"Wh…?"

"I saw the whole thing. I was on my way here when you threw him into the street. Very good by the way – remind me not to upset you in a hurry! He got up and staggered off just after you closed the door. He caught up with that woman you threw out just before him and they staggered off together to the park," he pointed out the path they took.

"The little bas…."

"It's alright Helen – I'm here now," his voice was low and sent a shiver down Helen's spine.

Again he tried to edge his way forward and Helen started to close the door on him.

"You still can't come in!" she insisted.

"Oh yes I can. You want me to, really," he nodded.

"I do NOT!" she shouted, and slammed the door with force.

In a state of panic, she immediately flicked the catch and threw the bolt at the top of the door as he started to knock loudly. She ran through to the kitchen and picked up the phone as she passed on her way to the back door. She checked and was relieved to find it locked. As soon as the operator spoke, she screamed to get the police. The librarian had started begging through the letterbox to be let in. He explained how much he loved her and tried to convince her that she really needed him, especially now she was single again. Helen was revolted by his comments. As she stood in the kitchen listening to him squirm his undying love for her she began to believe that he was actually quite pathetic and not as much of a threat as she had first thought. She almost pitied him and began to wonder if it had been worth calling the police over. Her initial panic had gone and taken all of her fear with it. He was still begging when Helen heard the sirens wail in the distance. Quickly, in his realisation, he said his goodbyes and apologised for his misdemeanour before the police car pulled up outside and the knock on the door came. Helen was comforted by WPC Jordan as she explained about the librarian and his sickening advances towards her. A second officer took notes. Jordan radioed in and had the man's name and address within minutes. She was assured that a patrol car would go to his address to question him. He would not be bothering Helen anymore.

"We will need to take a statement from you Miss Waters, regarding your sighting the other night. Would it be convenient for you to come down to the station now? We would like to speak with you about the incidents at St Anthony's too. Just routine you understand?"

Helen excused herself and hurried upstairs to get dressed. The two officers went outside to wait in their car and Helen joined them shortly after. WPC Jordan asked about Graham. How well did she know him? What was he like? What did she know about his relationship with Lucy? Helen could not answer the questions as fully as she would have liked because she had only seen him around and not really got to know him very well at all.

"Although he does seem odd," she began to explain, "he can be a real geek, sort of harmless, a bit nerdy, and then all of a sudden he goes… mad, like really aggressive."

Helen remembered the encounter with Graham in the Home when he had exploded. She paused and collected her thoughts as the car pulled into the station car park. The librarian was across the car park with two other officers. He saw Helen and shouted his apology over the roofs of the cars between them. One of the officers immediately grabbed his arm and dragged him aggressively in the opposite direction towards a black door in the far wall. Helen was ushered through two long corridors and into an interview room where DI Thompson joined her and WPC Jordan.

* * * * *

It was almost lunchtime when Helen returned home. She unlocked the door and entered the hallway with a long sigh, pulled off her shoes and threw her coat at the stand, which latched on at an awkward angle but managed to remain on the peg. She walked through to the kitchen and saw a large bunch of flowers on the worktop in front of her. There was a card poking out from the decorative foliage but she really did not want to read it.

"Too late Nathan. Too little too late."

She walked through to the sitting room without paying the flowers any more attention though she noticed out of the corner of her eye that the dining table had been set. She turned to see the best cutlery was laid out on her mother's old tablecloth with polished wineglasses and two tall, white candles in ornate holders. The silver glinted and the glass reflected the window giving the table a sparkle that made Helen smile. She tried not to be impressed but she had to applaud Nathan for this.

"That's better. I just hope you've bought take out and not attempted to cook!" she whispered.

"Nathan?" she called.

She walked through to the bottom of the stairs and looked up.

"Nathan?" she called louder.

Still smiling to herself she turned to the kitchen and headed for the kettle. As she stooped to get the milk from the fridge, she felt a dull thud on the back of her head. Slowly, her vision blacked over as her head grew warm and she fell to the cold floor. It was the strange sounds and the feeling of being moved that finally woke Helen. She realised that her mouth was covered before she was completely conscious but she still attempted to scream. The tape across her mouth wouldn't let the sound out; it bounced around in her mouth and made no impact on the outside world. Her head hurt; she could feel it throbbing. She opened her eyes wide in horror as she realised that her hands and feet were tied. Like a snared rabbit knowingly facing its final frantic moments, she wriggled instinctively to no avail.

"Nice of you to join us," said a voice from out of her line of sight, "we've been waiting for you."

With a heavy head of concussion, Helen realised she was upstairs in her own bedroom. She was laid on her side, looking out towards the window, with her hands taped together, as were her ankles. The evening was drawing in bringing a blue-grey darkness to the outside world, echoing the growing emptiness inside. She turned her head back and rolled over. When she saw Nathan, tied to the chair by the dressing table, she tried to scream. The scene was frighteningly familiar. She had imagined this before at the mercy of Tom. Nathan was only just conscious, bleeding heavily from a wound on his head and from his mouth. His head bobbed up and down like a cork on a pond as he made low, gargling sounds in his throat every time he drew his shallow breaths. The shadowy figure stood next to him lashed out and knocked Nathan's head back.

"I think my Grandfather would have liked this," he began, "he was a great lover of this game!"

He took hold of Nathan by the hair and held his head upright,

"How could you love a man such as this?" he shook his head.

"Did you know he was doing Lucy too? He called her 'Sunday Lunch'. Did you even suspect it? Every weekend while you were working. How does that feel? This man played you for a fool!"

He threw Nathan's head back again and Nathan let out a growled scream.

"He caught me up here. I only wanted you, sweet Helen, but then he turned up. He wanted to warn you, you know, but I couldn't let him spoil my fun," he sneered, "so I took this off him!" he threw something onto the bed.

Helen was sick into her mouth when she realised that what she was looking at was the severed end of Nathan's tongue, ripped, ragged and bloody. The man laughed through his nose, and laughed louder when he saw Helen begin to choke. He leaned forward and ripped the tape off her mouth in one quick movement. Helen spat the remaining bile out on the bed and took a deep breath before she started to scream. The screaming stopped almost instantly when his heavy fist made harsh contact with her temple bringing a quiet blackness to her senses.

* * * * *

DI Thompson stormed into St Anthony's Home, running through the reception hall and down the corridor to the staff room. All conversations stopped as he burst through the door. All faces stared with wide eyes and open mouths.

"Where's Helen Waters?" he demanded.

"She's at home; off sick. The stress had got to her and with Tom dying she just..." came the reply from a colleague sat on a couch sipping coffee.

Thompson didn't wait for a full explanation and flew out of the doorway as quick as he had appeared, leaving several startled women to gossip with each other about what may or may not be happening. Back in his car, he reversed off the forecourt without fastening his seatbelt, screeched into a turn and sped off in the direction of Helen's house. He radioed in to base and demanded back-up at her address. All available armed officers were to wait for him to arrive.

* * * * *

When Helen awoke, the world felt so abstract, as if confused and delirious, until slowly she realised that she was tied to the four corners of the bed and completely naked. She tried to scream and move but her arms and legs were stretched out and secured in place with Nathan's neckties and her mouth had been taped. She looked to Nathan who had stopped moving and had lost a lot of blood. All she could do was weep. Her heart was beating so fast it tripped over its own rhythm and bounced so hard through her chest it felt as if it were trying to break out. Pins and needles prickled down her arms and her limbs were cold and ached through being stretched to their maximum reach. Her stomach ached in its emptiness as it tried to create enough bile for her to reach but had no success. The shadowy figure stood at the foot of the bed. Helen realised that he was masturbating. She could hear the squelching noise of his actions and his breathing. Suddenly, she felt warm splashes across her feet as he groaned and then he sat on the edge of the bed. He was breathing heavily as he savoured the sights and smells and stroked her legs, rubbing his semen up and down her shins and massaging it into her ankles. She felt the warm fluid turn dry and cold. Helen thrashed her head from side to side, she tried so hard to pull her arms and legs close into her body but she could not get free. Her vulnerability was overwhelming and often she swooned in and out of focus. He laughed again and rose to his feet. Helen raised her head and looked directly at him. She could see nothing more than a glint in his eye through the slit in his balaclava. He was a looming shadow against the brightness of the landing light behind him and the dim grey of the fading natural light in the bedroom. She felt his hand stroke up her leg, round her knee and caress her thigh. Her stomach turned.

"Good girl," he whispered.

She thought of screaming but it seemed so pointless. She screwed her eyes tight and screamed in her mind. She visualised herself in a padded room, thrashing about at an unseen enemy, kicking and punching the walls, screaming, screaming, screaming. His hand moved towards her vagina and he gently stroked and invaded her. Ultimately vulnerable, her fear became insurmountable. His uninvited fingers pushed their way inside her heightening her disgust. She felt sick and her insides knotted. Pulling with her arms and getting nowhere, she wriggled on the bed but could not loosen the ties. The pins and needles had become a numbness; her hands and feet were no longer her own. She felt his fingers retreat as his tongue penetrated her. He took her knees in his hands and pushed them apart with just enough force to conquer her resistance. Feeling warm and wet, in a sickly, sluggish way, she writhed and squirmed on the bed. After some moments, he lifted his head, licked her stomach and made his way slowly up towards her breasts. He lingered, licked and kissed gently. Helen was sick again into her mouth and as soon as she felt the burning bitterness in her throat she began to choke, jolting her body and surprising her assailant.

"Bitch!" he spat and slapped her across the face.

Helen was fighting for breath and her face had turned red. She saw him stare at her for a moment with a fascinated look in his eyes. He faded in and out of view as her vision blurred over. Sharply, he pulled the tape off her mouth again but this time Helen continued to writhe. The pressure built up in her face, her eyes bulged in their sockets and her tongue protruded, as if trying to escape her blocked mouth. He reached out, untied her hands and slowly pulled her upright. With no effort to hurry, no sense of urgency, he slapped her hard between the shoulder blades: No reaction. He slapped her again and the bile flew from her mouth and splashed over his trousers.

"Jesus, woman!" he spat.

He threw her back down on the bed and slapped her across the face time and time again, throwing her face from one side to the other with the force. Helen's world slowly but surely became silent and dark. In pain, fear and absolute isolation, she thought she heard voices but she could have been wrong. Her one lingering thought as she drifted into unconsciousness was of St Anthony, looking down at her from the giant canvas, laughing.

* * * * *

DI Thompson waited outside Helen's house with seven armed officers looking in. The traffic in the street had been stopped as uniformed officers cordoned off the area. All lights on the cars had been switched off; all of the officers were watching the brightly-lit windows as they looked for signs of life. All along the row of houses opposite, neighbours looked out through pulled back curtains.

“All groups, standard initiation manoeuvres - go, go, go!” whispered the lead officer into his radio.

Figures in black ran along edges into shadows and took up their positions. Thompson ran up to the back door and paused with his back to the wall, his pistol pointed down towards the floor. He gave a series of hand signals that were passed from one officer to another; all were waiting, all were tense. Thompson took a step back from the door and two uniformed officers came forward. One officer took out a small drill and within seconds the lock was through and the door was pushed open. The officers moved quickly and quietly into the house and split off into rooms as they went. They pointed guns into corners and backed up to the walls. More officers had mirrored the procedures through the back door. The two teams congregated at the foot of the stairs. All eyes looked up and then at each other. After a couple of hand signals, Thompson went first, followed by his armed colleagues. He held his pistol in one hand, the other held flat against the wall. They all walked slowly, with steady, deliberate movements wrapped in caution; all eyes scanned their field of vision. They reached the top of the stairs and fanned out with their guns pointing forwards. Two officers slipped into one side room as another rolled back to the bathroom. The cautious detective went to the door in front of him and listened intently. He pushed the door wide and held his pistol in front of him with both hands.

Helen was laid on the bed; naked with her legs secured with ties. Unmoving, her body was smeared with blood and sweat. Nathan was strapped into a chair with his hands tied behind him, slumped forward with his forehead almost resting on his knees. There was a deep red puddle beneath the chair, a long gash along one side of his head that matted his hair with blood and his skull was exposed beneath the torn flesh. An officer went over to him and gently felt for a pulse in his neck. The officer shook his head in the direction of the detective. Another officer had reached out to Helen, looked at the detective and whispered,

"She's still alive, but only just - and not for long."

Officers were in and out of all the rooms. They opened cupboards and looked under beds. The house was empty and the lead officer declared it safe. The detective spoke into his radio and paramedics entered the house. Flashing blue lights lit the night alongside bright camera flashes blinking shadows across the walls. Uniformed officers from all services hurried back and forth as they carried out their duties with professional care. Helen's unconscious body was stretchered out, followed by Nathan's corpse, zipped tight in a black body bag.

* * * * *

He pushed his way through the turnstiles and walked quickly across the platform, looked left and right and boarded the train as it stood in the station. As he walked through the carriages he studied the passengers before he took a seat opposite a beautiful young oriental girl, travelling alone.

"Hello, mind if I sit here?" he said politely, as he pushed his glasses up on his nose.

www.ingramcontent.com/pod-product-compliance
Lightning Source LLC
LaVergne TN
LVHW091001080826
845145LV00003B/1083